# Mysterious Strangers

# Mysterious Strangers

**Dayle Courtney**

**Illustrated by
John Ham**

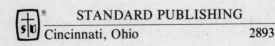
STANDARD PUBLISHING
Cincinnati, Ohio                    2893

*Thorne Twins* Adventure Books

Library of Congress Cataloging in Publication Data

Courtney, Dayle
  Mysterious strangers.

(Thorne Twins adventure books; 8)
  Summary: In trying to sort out the confusion caused by mysterious lookalikes in their hometown, Eric and Alison rely on their Christian principles when they find themselves involved with a strange scientist and an international spy ring.
  [1. Spies—Fiction. 2. Twins—Fiction. 3. Christian life—Fiction] I. Ham, John, ill. II. Title. III Series: Courtney, Dayle. Thorne Twins adventure books; 8.
PZ7.C83158My                    [Fic]                    82-3320
ISBN 0-87239-552-9                                       AACR2

# Contents

# 1 • The Police

From the breakfast table, Eric Thorne could see the rose garden his mother had tended so long ago. Her flowers were blooming more abundantly than ever. He wished she could see them now.

Across the table, Alison, his twin sister, was watching, too. A brindle cat strolled through the bushes and sniffed the strands of grass.

"I haven't seen him before," said Eric. "He must be new in the neighborhood."

"That must be the Carlsons' cat," said Alison. "Susie Carlson told me her grandmother gave it to her. Susie's mother isn't exactly overjoyed, but Susie just loves her new pet."

Eric smiled, remembering other cats and other days. "Mother always liked to have a cat around."

"Old Bearcat," said Alison. "Dad said he was the best mouser Mom ever had. I wish we knew what happened to him."

"He just got old and feeble and went off by himself, the way elephants in Africa are supposed to do."

Aunt Rose, the housekeeper, bustled up bowls of hot cereal, which she placed in front of the twins. "It's certainly good to have you both home again," she said. "I hope you'll stay a while this time. It seems like you're just never here any more. Always traipsing around the world to some awful place."

Alison laughed at her motherly scolding. "Blame that on Dad. He's the one that's been calling on us to help him with his assignments. But it's been a wonderful experience for us."

"Besides," added Eric, "it sure is nice getting out of school early!"

The doorbell rang as Aunt Rose turned back to the kitchen. "I'll get it," she called. "You eat your breakfast."

Eric spooned the hot cereal carefully and waited for it to cool. He glanced around the familiar ivory walls of the kitchen. It was an old-fashioned kitchen in an old-fashioned house. Dr. Thorne had changed it little since his wife died. Aunt Rose kept it in spotless condition and hired the painters and the carpenters and the plumbers to keep it in repair, but it still looked almost the same as when Elizabeth Thorne died.

Eric sometimes wondered if they shouldn't do some remodeling, bring their house up to date. They could do with new kitchen cabinets and fixtures. But their father was home so seldom, and Eric and Alison were gone much of the time, too. They simply never got around to it. But actually, Eric thought, he didn't want it changed. It was like a picture of the past, a past he wanted to remember very clearly. And besides, it was comfortable to live in the way it was.

He heard the distant voices of Aunt Rose and someone else—a man's voice—at the front door. "I wonder who that could be this early. Not many people know we're back home."

"Nobody but the fifty or so who were here for the welcome-home party they gave us last night," said Alison.

"Well, yeah—but I don't think any of them would be calling yet. They're probably still sacked out. It must have been nearly two A.M. when the last of them left."

"Three."

There was silence from the front of the house now, and then the sound of footsteps coming along the hall. Eric looked toward the door of the dining alcove, wondering.

A familiar figure appeared, one Eric hadn't seen for a long time. He arose quickly with outstretched hand. "Lieutenant Mitchell! It's good to see you."

The lieutenant never changed. His suits always appeared fresh from the cleaners, his shirts stiffly starched. His bulky figure sweat a lot, but he kept a tie firmly knotted about his neck during duty hours. His only sign of discomfort was a frequent wiping of his ruddy face and neck with a broad, white handkerchief.

He gave Eric his hand with what seemed a strange hesitation. "Hello, Eric," he said.

9

"Hi, Mr. Mitchell." Alison smiled and looked up at him.

The detective seemed to fumble for words. "It's good to see you young folks, too," he said, still avoiding their eyes. Finally he looked up. "I'm sure sorry to bother you this early in the morning, Eric, but we've got a little matter down at the office that we need your help on. I'd like you to come down with me."

"Right now?" Eric glanced back at his cooling breakfast.

"Yes. I hate to do this, but it's pretty important."

*How did the lieutenant even learn we were back in town?* Eric wondered. Of course, the families of all the friends who had visited last night were aware of it. News moves quickly in Ivy.

But Eric wondered what possible urgency would make Lt. Mitchell come looking for him at this time? He scanned the detective's round, weathered face more closely. Mr. Mitchell seemed deliberately unwilling to meet his gaze.

"Sure, I'll be glad to come," Eric said finally. "But can you tell me what this is all about?"

"I can do it easier down at the office." The lieutenant edged toward the door to the hall.

Aunt Rose bristled. "What in the world is so all-fired important that it can't wait a while, Ed Mitchell? These kids have only been home for a day, and they were up most of the night visiting with their friends."

"It shouldn't take long." The policeman's voice was genuinely apologetic.

10

"No problem." Eric forced himself to relax now. He patted Aunt Rose on the shoulder and smiled at Alison. "How about some fried eggs when I get back?" he said to the housekeeper.

"I think you're mean," Alison said to the officer.

They went out the front door while Alison and Aunt Rose watched with frowns of displeasure.

Going down the front steps, Lt. Mitchell said again, "We've got something strange that I just don't understand. I sure do need your help."

Eric tried to think what kind of problem his and Alison's return to Ivy might have created. Or what problems had preceded them from their recent journey? He could think of nothing.

"I'll be glad to help," he said. "I'll take my car and follow you."

"We'll drive you." The lieutenant's voice was like a command. "One of the patrolmen will bring you back." Eric glanced at him sharply but said nothing more.

He climbed in beside Ed Mitchell. Only then did he notice the officer in the back seat, a new man Eric didn't know. Lt. Mitchell introduced them and started the car. It was a couple of miles down the tree-lined Campus Avenue to the center of town.

As they passed the familiar streets, Eric remembered how it was when he was a ten-year old, how he used to wave to Ed Mitchell and all the other policemen in their big, shiny cars with the red and blue lights on top. And Ed and the others would wave back. Ed no longer patrolled the streets. Two or three years ago, he had been promoted to Detective Lieutenant, in charge of the Larceny Division.

The lieutenant seemed more at ease now. He asked Eric about his father. "Your dad and I used to spend a lot of time together as kids," he said. "I remember summers like this when we'd take the afternoon off from the grain elevator where we both worked. We'd get a load of guys in your dad's old jalopy and go swimming way over in Pike's Creek before they put the dam in. It was a big bunch of water then. Randall Thorne could outswim anybody in town."

"He's still a good swimmer," Eric said.

"He off on one of his consulting trips now?"

"In Sumatra until the end of the summer. Then he's got a couple of months in Burma."

"Must be great to see the world like that," the lieutenant sighed enviously. "I've never seen much but Ivy and a half dozen counties roundabout. I guess you and your sister have been seeing a lot of the world, too."

Eric listened absently to the detective's chatter. He couldn't keep from wondering about the purpose of this trip to the police station. Then he became suddenly alert.

"I guess you can get hold of your dad anytime you want to," the lieutenant was saying. "You keep in pretty close touch with him? Like if you wanted to call him on the phone this morning, you could?"

Lt. Mitchell was fishing for something or warning him. The implied meaning that Eric might *want* to reach his father tightened his stomach muscles.

Ed Mitchell stopped talking. He drove quietly until he reached the station. There he got out and led the way to the office in the front part of the building.

They passed the sergeant on duty at the front desk and went to a back room where three other men waited. A clerk, busy at his desk, an officer seated at one side of the room, and beside him a third man whom Eric instantly recognized. It was Sam Barrett, the owner of Barrett's Supermarket, the oldest store in town.

Sam Barrett had started out with a small grocery that Eric remembered from the time he was a very little boy. He and his friends had bought candy bars after school from Mr. Barrett. The storekeeper had been one of the boys' closest friends in those years.

He seemed to have become very old since Eric last saw him. His white hair was scattered thinly about his head. His eyes seemed to have sunk in their sockets above his wrinkled skin.

He glanced briefly and with apparent bitterness toward Eric, then turned sharply away. Eric was startled by his strange behavior. He smiled and extended a hand. Perhaps Sam Barrett had failed to recognize him.

"How are you, Mr. Barrett?" he said. "It's been a long time since we last saw each other. I sure do remember those candy bars you sold us kids at half price without ever telling us."

The old man kept his face turned away.

"Why don't you sit over here, Eric?" said Lt. Mitchell hastily.

Eric stared in puzzlement at his old friend, then sat

13

where the lieutenant indicated. "I hope you're ready to tell me what this is all about," Eric said.

"I think so." Lt. Mitchell turned to the storekeeper. "Now that Eric is here, why don't you go over your story again, Mr. Barrett? Let him hear it firsthand from you."

Sam Barrett shuffled his feet and looked down at the worn linoleum tile floor. "It's just like I told you. I came down to the store late last night to finish some inventory work. I couldn't sleep, and Martha wasn't feeling well enough to help me out today; so I decided to do it myself.

"As I drove into the parking lot to go in the back door, my lights showed a car standing there. I saw that a window next to the door had been broken open. It had bars, but they had been pried apart. Then, while I was getting out of my car, a person inside opened the door and ran out. In my lights, I could see him real plain— even though he tried to throw his arm up and hide his face. He was carrying a bag of some kind. He tossed that in the car—it was an old, green Chevy—and took off real fast."

His listeners waited for Sam Barrett to go on, but he stopped and glared at everyone in the room. He eyes came to rest on Eric.

"And did you recognize who it was?" The lieutenant's voice was gentle.

Sam Barrett nodded fiercely. His hands clenched in tight fists. "I saw him—plain as day. He didn't have any mask or hat or anything to hide him."

"And who was it?"

"You know who it was! I've already told you—it was him!" Sam Barrett half rose in fury and pointed a shaking finger at Eric. "It was Eric Thorne who robbed my store last night!"

For a moment, Eric scarcely comprehended what had happened. He seemed caught in a timeless space in which all eyes in the room were upon him, and nothing moved. No clocks ticking. No breathing. No hearts beating—not even his own.

He stood up, and time resumed. He took a step toward Sam Barrett. The old storekeeper looked at him defiantly.

"You're accusing me of breaking into your store?" Eric demanded.

"You heard me, Eric Thorne. I saw you just as I see you now. You took four hundred and eighty dollars out of my safe!"

Eric backed away and turned to Lt. Mitchell in stunned disbelief. "This doesn't make any sense at all! You all know me. You've known me all my life. You know I wouldn't do a thing like that. It's plain crazy! You've got to be mistaken, Mr. Barrett. You may have seen someone who resembled me—and I don't know who that could be—but you certainly didn't see me!"

Eric turned to each of the others in the room. There was embarrassed silence as they tried to look everywhere but at Eric. All except Sam Barrett. He continued to glare in bitter accusation.

"You believe me, don't you?" Eric exclaimed. A

feeling of desperation rose in him as they all seemed united against him in cold accusation. He faced Ed Mitchell. "Surely you don't think this crazy story could be true, do you?"

"Sit down, Eric," the lieutenant said quietly. "We certainly don't want to believe it. Can you tell us where you really were last night?"

Eric sat down. "Of course, I can. I was home."

"At about ten-fifteen?"

"Yes."

"Is there anyone who could testify that they knew you were home at that time?"

"About fifty people. All our old gang came over to give Alison and me a welcome-home party. Most of them were at our house from about nine o'clock until one or two. They could all tell you where I was at ten-fifteen."

Lt. Mitchell exhaled a long sigh of relief and smiled at Eric with genuine warmth for the first time that morning. He turned to Sam Barrett. "Well, Sam, that seems to take care of that. We can bring in some of those people if necessary and check Eric's story. Do you want to do that? Do you still want to press charges?"

The old man spread his hands in resignation. "What would be the use? Eric Thorne always was a clever boy. But I never thought he would do a thing like this. If he says he can bring in fifty witnesses to dispute my word, I'm sure he can. Nobody would believe old Sam Barrett. They wouldn't take my word against the respected *Eric Thorne* and all his friends."

He rose suddenly in renewed anger, his face red. He shook a bony finger in Eric's face. "But I know what I saw! And with my own eyes I saw you come out of my store with a bag of money and drive away. It was you, Eric Thorne. And nobody else!"

He sagged down into his seat once more.

"You want to press charges?" the lieutenant repeated. "You have the right."

"No. No charges. Nobody would believe old Sam Barrett." He turned on Eric in sadness now, his fury gone. "I don't see how you could do this to me. I don't see how you could turn out to be a common burglar. I need that money. Won't you give it back to me?"

Eric touched the old man's arm. "I haven't got your money. I swear I haven't. But if there's a thief around town who looks like me, I want to know who it is just as much as you do. I want to help find the burglar and get your money back for you, Mr. Barrett."

The storekeeper arose and shook off Eric's hand and moved toward the door. "I don't need your kind of help. I just don't ever want to see you again. Keep out of my store—you and all your clever friends."

He moved slowly out the door of the office, hunched over in misery. Eric started toward him, but the lieutenant held him back. "Let him go, Eric. He's pretty upset."

"Well, so am I!" Eric retorted. "I want to get to the bottom of this!"

"It's simply a case of mistaken identity. Sam's eyesight isn't what it used to be. He couldn't see much last night with just the lights of his car. We'll work on it and let you know.

"I'm sorry we had to trouble you this morning, but if we'd waited longer, Sam would have sworn out a complaint and we would have had to arrest you. I was pretty sure his accusation wouldn't hold up once I got you two together. An officer will drive you home."

"I want to help," Eric insisted. "It's my concern, too, if this burglar looks enough like me to be mistaken for me."

"We'll keep in touch. We'll let you know what turns up."

"Sure." It was obvious to Eric that Ed Mitchell didn't want help of any kind from him. "Sure," he repeated. "Thanks, Mr. Mitchell."

He walked out with one of the newer officers, Tom Coleman, who drove him home. Neither of them had anything to say.

Alison was waiting impatiently for him. "I thought the police had locked you up," she said.

"They almost did."

"What?"

Eric told her the story of his encounter at the police station. When he was through. Alison's face was tense, but she forced a laugh.

"We'll have to get Mr. Barrett some new glasses," she said.

"It's no laughing matter. Think how it could have turned out if no one had known where I was last night."

"It could have become complicated." Alison

continued to try to force a smile. She was upset by Eric's story. "But I would have been your character witness."

"You would have been a character, period. I'd sure like to meet up with that guy that robbed the store—and who Sam Barrett thinks looks like me."

"We ought to do something to help Mr. Barrett get his money back."

Eric shook his head. "He doesn't want us anywhere near him. Besides, Dad wants us in Argentina in two weeks."

"I know. We'll—"

The ringing of the telephone interrupted her. "I'll get it," she said.

She went to the hall phone, and Eric heard her answer. "Yes. He's not in, now. This is she."

There was a long silence. Then Alison replaced the phone quietly and came back to the living room.

"That was a lively conversation," said Eric.

Alison didn't answer. She remained standing in silence in the center of the rug in front of the fireplace. Her face was pale.

Eric jumped to his feet and strode to her. "Alison! What is it?"

Her voice was small, like a little girl's. "I'm scared, Eric. I'm really scared."

"Of what? What was that call?"

"Sheriff Rayburn, over in Midland."

Eric remembered him, too. A friendly man who had been sheriff a long time in the next county. "Well, what did he say to scare you? We seem to be doing an awful lot of business with police this morning.''

"It's not funny, Eric!'' Alison pressed her clenched fists against her cheeks. "I tell you I'm scared. Mr. Rayburn wants me to come right over and see him.''

"Why?''

"He said he's holding a man in his jail right now for burglary. He said it's my brother, Eric Thorne!''

# 2 • A New Twin

Midland was twenty-three miles from Ivy. The town had been by-passed by the interstate, and the road from Ivy was worn and rough. Nevertheless, Midland was the county seat, and a lot of traffic moved over the narrow road. Eric let the cars pass him. He drove slowly between the rich blackness of the freshly plowed fields.

His slow driving irritated Alison. "Let's go faster. We'll never get there at this rate."

"I'm trying to think what we're going to do when we get there. What are you supposed to say to a person who's in jail for burglary and who has been identified as you?"

"We want to know who he is. That's what. Has he actually been using your name, or do people just think he looks like you?"

"I guess I *am* making too much of this." Eric felt an anger at himself. "Getting all jittery just because some character who looks like me has been robbing stores.

We'll find out who he is and straighten the whole thing out and then forget about him. Right?''

"Sure. It just kind of shakes you up to run into something like this. Two weeks from now, we'll be in Buenos Aires, and this will seem as if it never happened." Alison was suddenly more cheerful, and Eric felt good about that. He wondered why he didn't feel cheerful, too.

Midland, a small and usually quiet town, was humming with activity. The elevators, north of town, did a big business this time of year, dispensing seed, fertilizer, and spray chemicals. While they were in town, the farmers tried to do some quick shopping for other goods, as well. Cars lined the streets. Midland was considering parking meters.

"There's the city hall." Alison pointed to a small spire a couple of blocks off Main Street. Eric headed for it, at the same time telling himself this was all a very minor matter that would be resolved in a few minutes.

They parked in the shade of one of the few trees scattered in the small block behind the building. Eric noted a small sign hanging from an iron bracket: *Sheriff's Office*. He took Alison's arm and strode purposefully toward the doorway.

A counter was just inside, so close it was impossible to squeeze by when the door was open. Eric let the door fall shut behind them. The room had a typical city-hall smell.

From behind the counter a deputy at a desk looked up without interest. "Help you folks?"

"Sheriff Rayburn, please," said Eric. "He's expecting us. The Thornes."

The deputy leaned back to peer through the open door at the opposite side of the room. He could see no one. He reached for the phone.

There was no need. A shadow suddenly appeared in the doorway, and then the bulky figure of Sheriff Rayburn. He was absently brushing back the wisps of long gray hair that lay across his otherwise bald head.

He stopped and stared. Then he scuttled between the desks to cross the room. He leaned his big hands on the counter and stared again at Alison and Eric.

"Alison—I talked to you on the phone just a while ago. And this—" He looked at Eric in total stupefaction, then turned to glance at another open door that led to the hall, and, obviously, to the cells of the small jail.

"You—he—" Sheriff Rayburn turned back to them. "I don't understand what's going on," he said finally.

"Neither do we," said Eric. "I understand you told my sister you had me in a cell here in your jail."

"I do! I *did*—Then who the dickens is that fellow? He's the spittin' image of you. I've known you since you were a little boy, Eric, but I would have sworn that fellow was you."

"Well, he isn't. I am, and I'd like to know who *he* is. You see, we've run into him—or a story about him—once before this morning." He told Sheriff Rayburn about the robbery of Sam Barrett's store.

"It was like that here," said Sheriff Rayburn. "He broke into a store about four o'clock this morning.

23

Would have got away, too, except that old Mike Staggs was going in early to do some paperwork at the grainery. He spotted this fellow climbing out a window and called the office from that phone down by Art Miller's gas station. Luckily, Dave Bell—you wouldn't know him—was in the patrol car about a block away. Bell nabbed him before he had time to get that old wreck of a car of his started."

"A green Chevy?" said Eric.

"Yeah. How'd you know? No license plates. No registration."

"Sam Barrett saw the same car by his store."

The sheriff took a deep breath. "Well—what's next? You want to see this fellow? Somehow, we've got to find out who he really is."

"We may as well," said Eric. He really didn't want to see this impersonator, he thought. He wished whoever it was would just go away, disappear somehow.

"Come on out this way." The sheriff opened a gate in the counter and led them through the room to the door opening on the hall. At the far end were the steel bars of the four jail cells. Only one was occupied.

The prisoner was seated on the dirty mattress of the bunk bed that swung down from the wall and was supported by chains. He had his face down, supporting his head in his hands. His coat was off, hanging on a hook by the dirty wash basin. His shirt was rumpled and soiled. To Eric, he was a picture of dejection.

The sheriff's voice boomed out, "Hey, there. You got some visitors, fella."

24

The young man looked up slowly, as if not wanting to be disturbed. But he seemed not at all surprised to see Eric and Alison. It was as if he'd been expecting them. Without speaking, he got up from the dirty bunk and walked toward them. He put his hands on the bars, leaning at arm's length against them.

His eyes scanned Eric's face. "I'd heard about you," he said finally.

"Who are you?" asked Eric.

"I'm Eric Thorne."

Eric couldn't suppress being startled by the simple, matter-of-fact statement. "I've been wearing that name for the past sixteen years," said Eric.

"You do have to admit we look alike, don't you?"

"Yes. But that doesn't make you me."

The prisoner hung his head as he leaned against the bars. His eyes focused on the floor. "It doesn't make me anybody," he said with a frightening bitterness.

Eric said to Sheriff Rayburn, "Can we go somewhere and sit down to talk?"

The sheriff looked doubtful, as if this were something much too irregular.

"We need to try to figure this thing out," Eric said.

The sheriff rattled his keys and fitted one to the lock. "All right. You can take that small office next to mine." To the prisoner he said warningly, "Good behavior, now. Got it?"

"Sure, Sheriff. I'm always on my very best behavior."

The sheriff guided them to the room and left them,

27

but Eric noticed he was keeping a watchful eye from behind his desk in his own office, to which the door remained open. There was no way out of the room except through the sheriff's office.

The prisoner spoke. "I guess you want to know who I am—besides Eric Thorne. Where I came from and all that."

"You've got me into some embarrassing situations with the Ivy Police and now with Sheriff Rayburn."

The prisoner laced his fingers on the table and rubbed his thumbs absently together. "I'm sorry about that. I was out of money and didn't know what to do. I'm not a very good burglar, you know."

"You got away from Barrett's with a sizable amount."

"Not nearly enough. How long could I last on that much?"

"You could get a job."

"And people would ask the same questions you want answers to. Who am I? Where did I come from? Where did I go to school? What was my last job? And the answer to all those questions is simply the same: I don't know."

"You mean you don't remember your past?" Alison spoke for the first time.

The prisoner nodded. "I can't remember. I can go back as far as when I was driving that car—I don't even know where I got it—toward the store last night. It occurred to me that I could break in and maybe get the money I badly needed."

"You remember nothing before that? Nothing of the day that just passed?"

The double spread his hands. "Nothing."

Eric leaned back and scanned the other's face intently. The claim to amnesia was just another unbelievable factor in the already complex mystery. It could be a complete lie.

But what would he, himself, do in such circumstances? Eric wondered. This person who looked so much like him—did he also *think* like him? This idea increased Eric's discomfort.

"Look," the double said. He leaned forward now, dropping his air of independence and arrogance. His voice appealed for understanding. "If you found yourself in such a position, how would you handle it? Suddenly you're nobody—but you must have been somebody at some time. All I remembered was the name, Eric Thorne. That's what I had been called."

"By whom?" said Alison.

"I don't know! I looked about the streets in the night. The lights showed me faces, but they were all faces of strangers. I knew none of them. I didn't know myself. I had no money. I was hungry. I knew I needed money to buy what I needed, but I didn't know any way to earn some. I had to take it. I'm sorry it involved you." His voice carried a note of genuine regret.

"I sympathize with your situation," said Eric. "But none of this helps understand who you are and where you came from—and how you and I are the very image of each other."

29

"If you could help me"—the stranger said. "If you could just give me a hand until I can find out who I am. I'm not a criminal. I was just so desperate—"

Eric nodded to Alison. "Let's talk to the sheriff." To the stranger he said, "Hang on. We'll be back in a few minutes."

Outside the room, Alison said in a low voice, "What are you going to do?"

"As he says, we all need to know who he is and where he came from. *I* want to know where he came from—wearing my face! If the sheriff will let him go, let's take him back to the house to stay with us for a while."

"Oh, Eric—"

"What?"

"Do you think we should?" Alison's fear rose again as she looked back at the stranger with his face turned away from them. "How can we trust him? We know nothing about him."

"I think we have to trust him, for at least a little way. Otherwise, we'll never find out anything about him. I really think he's telling the truth when he says he's not a criminal and was just desperate in breaking into those two stores."

"I can't help being afraid of the idea. But if you think it's all right—"

"Let's talk to Sheriff Rayburn."

The sheriff had been watching them from the corner of his eye. He looked up as they approached. "Well, what kind of a story did he give you?"

Briefly, Eric told the sheriff of their conversation, then said, "We'd like to take him home with us and see if this question of mixed-up identity can be straightened out. He *is* like an identical twin of mine. There's got to be some explanation for that."

The sheriff looked thoughtful. "Maybe you won't like what you find out."

"What do you mean by that?" asked Alison.

"Nothing in particular. Just that it's a pretty weird set of circumstances when you stop to think about it—his looking exactly like Eric, turning up in Ivy and then here in Midland just when you two get back from a long trip, robbing a couple of stores. I don't know. I think you're taking a big risk. Maybe too big."

"Can you release him to us?" asked Eric.

"I'll have to check with Bob Thomas, the county attorney, on that. He may not like it."

The sheriff dialed a call to another part of the building. When he reached Mr. Thomas, it was obvious the attorney was not in favor of the idea.

"Let me talk to him," whispered Eric.

The sheriff nodded reluctantly, listened, and said, "I'll put Eric on. He can tell you how he feels."

Mr. Thomas said, "Hello, Eric. I understand you want to take custody of this fellow that broke into a couple of stores last night."

Quickly, Eric outlined his reasons. "It's not as if we're asking for the release of an ordinary burglar. This fellow is amnesiac. He's in need of food and lodging. And besides, as the sheriff told you, he's the identical twin image of me, and he's carrying my name. It's crazy, but it's true. I've got to find out what's going on!''

Mr. Thomas spoke very precisely. "It sounds as if a proper investigation by suitable authorities, both legal and medical, needs to be carried out.''

"But is that going to happen, Mr. Thomas? We don't have the facilities in Midland or Ivy. It just won't get done. He'll sit in jail awhile and then maybe get a long sentence and go to State—and I'll never find out about him.''

"I gather this means a great deal to you.''

"It certainly does!''

The county attorney cleared his throat with a dignified cough. "It's against my better judgment. But what you say is true, of course. We haven't the facilities or money for a proper investigation. I'll give you temporary custody if he guarantees to stay at your place. And I'll bring him back here instantly if he moves one tick out of line. O.K.?''

"Thanks, Mr. Thomas. Thanks a lot!''

When Eric put the phone down, Sheriff Rayburn looked sourly at the twins. "He had no legal authority to do that, you know. We all could get in a big peck of trouble over this.''

32

# 3 • *More Surprises*

The ride back to Ivy was quiet. The stranger sat in the back seat and watched the landscape intently. Occasionally, he asked a question about the fields between which they rode. Alison answered.

As they came to the outskirts of Ivy, Alison gave a sudden exclamation. "We forgot all about Mr. Mitchell. He'll be looking for—'him'—too." They suddenly became aware, also, that they hadn't figured out a way to tell anyone about Eric and his strange twin.

"We'll need to get Mr. Mitchell's approval," said Alison. "And I don't think he's going to be as willing to give it as Mr. Thomas and Sheriff Rayburn."

"I think you're right," Eric said. He turned to the stranger. "You understand what she's saying? We're in a different county here. In addition, Ivy has its own Municipal Police Department. Lieutenant Mitchell may want to throw you in *his* jail and keep you there."

"I understand. I can give the money back."

"Do you have it?"

"They took it away from me at the other place. Most of it was there, except what I spent for some hamburgers."

Eric looked at Alison. "We'll have to get that squared away later and return it to Mr. Barrett. For now, I think we won't let Mr. Mitchell know you're here," he said to the stranger. "You're going to be out of sight, anyway."

The stranger nodded agreement. "I'll do whatever is necessary. Perhaps later I can get clearance from your police."

"We'll work on that when the time comes."


Eric steered the car into the drive beside the white frame house. The gables needed paint, he thought. And what about their trip to Buenos Aires? Sheriff Rayburn's words kept running through his mind: "We could all get in a big peck of trouble over this."

He hoped the sheriff was a very poor prophet.

They went in the back way to keep the stranger from being observed by the neighbors. But they had forgotten about Aunt Rose. She was in the kitchen polishing the floor when they entered. She shouted at them, "Keep off the wax!"

Then she looked up. She stared a moment while Eric realized their goof. He tried to say something. The housekeeper didn't hear anything he said. She simply collapsed into a chair and wiped the sudden perspiration from her brow. She swallowed and tried to speak.

"*Two* of you! *Two*—am I out of my mind?"

Eric hustled his companion through the door into the hall and up the stairs while Alison sat down and began to talk to Aunt Rose.

Eric led the way to one of the unused bedrooms with windows to the rear of the house. It was a large, well-lighted room that had been kept as a spare bedroom for visits of Mrs. Thorne's innumerable relatives. Aunt Rose kept it as it had been in the days of Eric's mother.

"You can use this room," Eric said.

"Who was that woman?" his companion asked.

"Who? Oh—Aunt Rose, the housekeeper. We'd forgotten all about her seeing you. Alison will take care of her. You'll need some clothes. I've got some spare things you can use. I'll get you soap and razor and toothbrush. Just take it easy and we'll talk later."

"Do you have any books?"

"Books? What kind?"

"Most any kind. Science, history, politics—things like that."

"My father has a huge library downstairs. I'll show it to you later. You're welcome to browse in it all you like. And, by the way, we've got to figure out what to call ourselves. We can't both be just Eric."

"I like that name."

"Yeah, me, too. We'll get it straightened out eventually, but for the time being, I'll be Eric One and you be Eric Two. Maybe Alison and Aunt Rose can call us One and Two, just to keep things from getting too jumbled."

"I could be One and you, Two."

"Well, let's just say that this is my house; so I'll be Eric One. When you find out where you came from and get off on your own again, you can be anything you like. O.K.?"

"Sure. That's fine. Two, it is."

"So why don't you relax a bit, and I'll rummage up some clothes. You'll probably want to take a bath and clean up a bit. We'll have dinner in an hour or so."

Eric met Alison in the living room. The sound of the floor polisher was heard again from the kitchen. "You get her squared away?" Eric motioned in the direction of the housekeeper.

Alison nodded. "She doesn't know what to make of all this, but her blood pressure is coming back down. I don't know if we can keep her quiet or not. Everything go all right upstairs?"

"Yes. It's O.K." Eric slumped down in the old vinyl reclining chair they had bought for their father long ago. "I feel as if I've really been through the wringer today. Is this all for real, or are we imagining it?"

"I'm afraid it's real enough." Alison was opening an envelope she had carried into the room and now was frowning over its contents.

"What's that?" said Eric.

"Aunt Rose said it came in this afternoon's mail. I don't understand it."

"What does it say?"

"It's a check from Lowry's Department Store."

"Refund for something?" said Eric.

"No. A paycheck."

"Must be sent to the wrong place. Who's it for?"

"Me. It's made out to Alison Thorne."

"So when did you work for Lowry's?"

"I didn't, dummy. You know that."

Eric shrugged. "Their computer's fouled up. It happens all the time. Send it back to them."

Alison dropped it on the end table by the sofa. "I'll be passing there in the morning. How are we going to get things squared away in time to make the schedule to Buenos Aires?"

After dinner, Two asked to see the library Eric had mentioned. When he saw it, he was like an excited child at the county fair. He drew volumes one by one from the shelves and opened them carefully as if they were precious objects of art.

"There are so many!" he exclaimed. "Do you mind if I read them?"

"Which ones do you like best?" Eric asked.

"All of them! I'll read them all! I don't want to miss any."

"That could take a while. I hope we have our other problems solved before you have time to go through all these. But help yourself. I'll show you how they are arranged."

Later, Eric and Alison finally went upstairs to bed, leaving Two in the library. He sat on the floor by the shelves, turning pages furiously as if he could absorb their contents at a glance.

At the top of the stairs, Alison stopped and looked

back to the light seeping into the stairwell from the library. "He's like a child with those books," she said slowly to Eric. "And yet there's a craftiness about him that still frightens me."

"You're imagining things."

"No, I'm not. I think if he ever finds out who he is—or was—we aren't going to want him around. He's been something—something horrid. And I think he still is. We've got to do whatever we're going to do with him and get him out of here. I can't stand having him around very long."

In his room, Eric couldn't wipe out of his mind Alison's misgivings. He admitted to himself he also felt uneasy. It was Two's absolute identity to himself that Eric could not put down. During the afternoon and evening, he had examined Two as closely as possible. Eric Two had a mole on the right side of his neck, which was exactly the same shape, size, and location as the one Eric had. Two's right ear was just slightly turned out from his head farther than his left. So was Eric's. There was a tiny wart on the back of his left hand. Eric had one there.

He had noted a dozen other minute similarities. Identical twins seldom had such precisely matching characteristics.

A frightening thought occurred to him—*What about fingerprints? Even identical twins do not have the same fingerprints. But what if he and I should have like prints? No. It's impossible—I think!*

He slept in spite of his fitful imaginings. But not too

long. He was up early and went downstairs before Alison or Aunt Rose had wakened. In the library, he found Two seated in the midst of scattered books. At least a hundred were piled in stacks around him.

"You been here all night?" Eric asked in amazement.

Two grinned apologetically. I guess I have. I just couldn't stop. Besides, I remembered what you said about time. I got through this many, but I'm afraid I can't get them back in the right places on the shelves."

"Wait a minute!" Eric knelt down beside Two. "Are you telling me you've read all these?"

"It was kind of slow going. I'm not used to reading much, but I got through this many."

"You *read* them?"

"Yes—I hope you don't mind." Two looked puzzled now. "Is something wrong?"

"No. No—not at all. But you must be a pretty fast reader."

"I didn't think so, but I'm glad you do."

Eric stood up. "Yeah—I *do* think so. You're a very fast reader. But don't you need some sleep now?"

He watched Two ascend the stairs and then turned back to count the books on the floor. There were a hundred twelve. Two had to be lying, or else he was some kind of genius.

Alison and Aunt Rose came down shortly. Eric told his sister about finding Two sitting among the books, but he refrained from telling her of Two's claim to have read a hundred twelve of them.

"Sleep O.K.?" he asked.

Alison nodded and pointed out the window. "There's that cat again. Seems like a million years since we noticed him in the rose garden. Was it only yesterday?"

"Only yesterday."

"What have you figured out—about 'him'?"

" 'Him' is Two. We agreed he would be Two and I would be One. That's as far as I've gone."

Alison sniffed. "Clever. Why didn't you just use your Social Security numbers?"

"He probably doesn't even have one."

"Everybody that old has to have one. And that's how we can track down who he is!"

Eric shook his head. "You can bet Sheriff Rayburn thought of that."

"Then why don't we just turn him over to a welfare agency?"

"Because he's my double, that's why." Eric told her about his observations and his suspicions about their fingerprints. "If he's got the same prints as I have, I'm going to be climbing the walls."

Alison sat down at the breakfast table and stared out at the meandering cat. "That would be scary, wouldn't it?"

Alison planned a shopping trip that morning. She took the car at about ten o'clock and decided to visit Lowry's first. She liked shopping there. Many of the girls who worked there were friends from high school.

The store was in one of the older buildings of Ivy. Its cast-iron front carried the date of its erection, 1886. But it had been carefully restored to reflect the comfortable, easy-going days when the town was young and full of hope. The building still made Lowry's customers feel at ease.

Alison parked in front and walked through the massive doors, their aged, carved dignity carefully refurbished. She remembered how fascinated she had been as a little girl to run her fingers over the carved snouts of the lions that graced the corners of the panels. She paused now and smiled as she touched the familiar images.

Inside, the smell of fabric and wood paneling was pleasant. She stopped at the perfume counter to talk with an old acquaintance, Mary Lou Haskins. They hugged each other and talked of the last year of school. Since the twins had finished the school year early to join their father in Sumatra in March, it had been a while since Alison and Mary Lou had seen each other.

"I guess I want to see the payroll department, Mary Lou," said Alison. "Can you tell me where it is?"

"Sure. Right up the middle stairs in back. Turn left and go in the office at the end of the hall. Janice is there. She got promoted last week. You remember Janice Holmes, don't you? That senior girl in freshman Home Ec. class."

"O.K. Thanks, Mary Lou. I'll drop in again."

Alison ran up the steps, trying to remember Janice Holmes. The buzz of morning customers on the main floor below died away as she followed the hall to the open door at the end. There was a small office filled with accounting machines and files and desks and three girls, including Janice Holmes, who was obviously in charge of the office. Alison remembered her now.

She came over at once. "Alison! It's so good to see you again."

"It's nice to be back." Alison glanced around. "It looks as if you're doing all right."

"I love it! They just moved me over here a week ago."

Alison opened her purse. "I guess I should give this to you. It came to the house yesterday. Eric says your computer must be fouled up."

"Oh—let me see."

Janice Holmes took the check and scanned it. "I don't see anything wrong with it, Alison. Isn't the amount right?"

"I don't know. It's made out to me."

"Yes. It's for the three days you worked week before last. Ellen said you weren't coming back and told me just to mail it out to you. Isn't that all right? Alison—what's wrong? Alison—you look as if you're going to faint. Sit down here. Are you all right?"

There was a terrible churning in Alison's stomach. It seemed for a moment as if the walls of the room were receding and leaving her stranded in a black void.

She clutched the edge of the desk and closed her eyes to steady herself. "I'm all right," she said finally, her voice weak. "But, Janice—I *didn't* work here that week or any other week."

She knew at once she shouldn't have said that.

Janice Holmes looked at her strangely. "I don't un-

42

derstand, Alison. You were in Ellen Grow's Junior Dresses for over six weeks. I saw your checks go out to Ellen's department. Didn't you get them? Alison— please sit down. You look so pale."

Alison accepted the chair beside Janice's desk. The tightening and churning in her stomach wouldn't go away.

Janice said brightly, "Why, here's Ellen now. I'll ask her if your checks didn't come through O.K."

Alison stopped her. "No. No—Janice. Everything's fine now. I just felt dizzy for a minute. I'm all right. Really."

Ellen Grow, a motherly, gray-haired supervisor in Junior Dresses, stopped and came into the office when she saw Alison. She clapped her hands on Alison's shoulders. "My dear! It's good to see you again. Are you coming back with us? Things haven't been the same in Junior Dresses since you left."

Alison looked up weakly. Her vision seemed blurred. She remembered Ellen Grow, a kindly, gentle woman. "No—I'm sorry. I can't come back just now. You see—I'm not feeling too well."

"Yes, I know. That's what you said when you left. I was so hopeful everything would be all right," Ellen Grow sympathized.

Alison passed a shaky hand over her face. "I don't know. Sometimes I can't remember things. I just can't remember how long—you say it was six weeks, Janice?"

Ellen Grow said, "That's right dear. Six weeks and

43

three days. Oh, I'm so sorry you haven't been well. I'm sure it wouldn't be good for you to come back just now. Did you go to Dr. Middleton as I suggested? He's so good. He gave me a nerve tonic last spring that just did wonders for me.''

Alison escaped at last, declining offers to have someone drive her home. She got into her car in front of the store, aware the two women were watching. She couldn't stop the pounding in her head and the sick contraction of her stomach. She backed the car out and was greeted with the furious honking of someone who had to swing out to avoid her. She shook her head to try to clear it and turned the car toward home.

She left the car in the driveway and stumbled into the house, calling for Eric.

Aunt Rose met her in the hall. "Eric's upstairs in his room. Alison—what is it?"

"I'm all right," Alison said desperately. "I just need to see Eric. I need to see Eric right away!"

She hurried up the stairs, half stumbling on every other step. She burst into Eric's room, where he was making some notes on a pad.

"Eric! Eric—it's happened again!" she sobbed.

He ran to her and put his arm around her. "What, Sis? What in the world has happened again?"

She raised her tear-stained face and looked at him in fright. "Just like it was with you, Eric. There's another me! There's another Alison Thorne here in town!"

# 4 • *Professor Swykert*

Alison and Eric sat in the shady gazebo at the back of the garden. Aunt Rose had prepared some tea, and it had quieted Alison's stomach somewhat. But she couldn't completely shake the panic that had seized her at the store.

"We've got to call Dad and tell him," Alison said. "Exact duplicates of both you and me here in Ivy—it just can't be some coincidence. There's something behind it."

"Sis—there's got to be a reasonable explanation. And these people: Eric Two and the girl who looks like you—they haven't done anything frightening. I'd say Eric Two is more frightened than we are. And I'll bet your double is the same. That's probably why she left the job. She heard the news that we were coming back."

"But *who* can she be? And Eric Two? We haven't learned anything yet."

45

Eric patted her hand. It was cold although the air was warm. "We haven't been on it very long," he said. "Our next step is to find this girl and see what she can tell us. But she may have left town by now."

"I don't want to find her!"

"Then we'll never solve the mystery of her existence, will we?"

"Oh, Eric—"

After a moment Alison straightened up and shook her head as if to clear her vision. "I'm sorry, Eric. I'm such a goon about this. It was a real shock to learn that I have a double, too. But I think I know now what the answer could be."

"What?" said Eric.

"Suppose that we weren't just twins when we were born. Suppose we were quadruplets. Four of us, not just you and me. These other two *are* our identical twin brother and sister."

Eric raised his hands in the air as if to ward off such a possibility. "There are a thousand explanations more reasonable than that."

"Name one."

"It would mean that Mom and Dad—well, what would it mean? They did something to put the others out of their lives. Can you imagine their doing that? Not in a million years! If there had been a litter of ten of us, they would have kept us all. They wouldn't have put some of us with anybody else—anywhere else."

"Shall we call Dad tonight and ask him?"

"No!"

"Think about it, Eric. It's the most plausible answer of all. There were four of us. Two have been somewhere else all these years, and now they've just turned up. I don't believe that amnesia story at all. I'm going to make Eric Two tell where he's been and what he's up to."

Eric waved a hand again in protest. "Take it easy. I can check the Department of Vital Statistics and see what record they have on our birth."

"No," said Alison. "It wouldn't be there."

"It would have to be. All vital statistics were recorded at the time we were born."

"They would have seen to it that it wasn't. Doctor Crawford would have been persuaded not to report more than two births."

"You're making Mom and Dad sound like a couple of dark and devious conspirators—getting the records falsified, hustling two of us off to some unknown destination. You're as balmy as a summer breeze."

"I am not!" Alison persisted. "Mom wasn't well for a long time after we were born. Dad wasn't making much money then. Four babies all at once would have been a disaster. They could easily have concluded two of us would have been better off in another home. Remember, too, we were born at home. With the doctor's assistance, there would have been no publicity."

"And old Dr. Crawford is long dead."

"And so is his nurse, Mrs. Doran. There's nothing left to prove the truth of the situation. Every track is buried."

"All but one." Eric shook his head.

"What?"

"Mom and Dad just weren't capable of something like that! You're miles off the beam. There's got to be a far more reasonable explanation."

"All right," said Alison firmly. "So it's your turn. Tell me the answer. In the end, we'll find I'm right. We've got a sister and a brother we've never known anything about."

Aunt Rose called from the back door. "Eric! Telephone."

"All right. Who is it?"

"Ed Mitchell. I hope he isn't going to cause any more trouble."

"Yeah, me, too," Eric said under his breath. To Alison he said, "You wait here. I'll see what he wants and be right back."

The detective's voice was less than friendly. "Eric, I hear from Matt Rayburn that you've got that fellow Sam Barrett thought was you."

Eric swallowed. "Yes, Lieutenant. Mr. Rayburn was kind enough to give us custody—with Mr. Thomas' approval—to see if we could find out something about who he is."

"You're taking a big chance. You're not equipped to restrain a criminal. What if he tries to escape? If Matt Rayburn doesn't want him in his jail, I sure do want him in ours."

"Mr. Barrett's money is safe." Eric felt a sudden desperation. "He only bought a couple of hamburgers.

We'll make that up to Mr. Barrett. Lieutenant," he pleaded, "we've *got* to find out about this. It's driving me and Alison out of our minds."

"I don't like it. You should have at least let me know, Eric."

"Yes, I should have. But I was afraid you would take him away from us."

"Legally, he's still Matt's prisoner," the lieutenant replied. It sounded like a concession he wasn't happy about. For a moment, he was silent. Eric heard his heavy breathing. Finally, he said, "But if he acts up, we're going to slap him right back in jail."

"Sure, I understand, Mr. Mitchell." Eric exhaled in relief. "I sure do appreciate your willingness to help us."

"That isn't what I called about mostly, however. Matt and I got together and traced that old car this fellow was driving around with no plates and no registration. We found where it came from—or who last owned it, anyway."

Eric wondered what this information had to do with him.

"It was last registered," said Lt. Mitchell, "about five years ago to Hamilton R. Swykert. You knew him, didn't you? Wasn't that old Professor Swykert who used to be up at the university? Didn't he and your father used to be good friends?"

Eric's memory tracked back over the years. He remembered the old fellow with whom his father used to spend hours in the library of their house. White haired.

Thin. Stooped even then. But a mind that kept Dr. Thorne's racing to keep up.

"Yes," Eric said. "He and my father were good friends once. I remember him faintly, but I haven't seen him for years. I imagine he must be dead by now."

"Could be. We checked, but there's no record of his death. Is there anything else you can tell us about him?"

"Not much. I was ten or twelve years old when he used to come to the house and talk with Dad for hours. I didn't know what they were talking about. I imagine this car is simply one that Swykert junked or abandoned, and my double got hold of it somehow. If you're looking for any significant connection between him and Swykert, I think you're mistaken."

"I suppose you're right," said the lieutenant. "I thought it might lead to something. Well, thanks for the information, Eric. And keep an eye on that fellow you've got over at your place. I still think jail is the place for him."

"I'll watch. And I'll sure call you if anything gets out of line."

He hung up and returned to the garden, where Alison still sat in the shade of the gazebo. "Are we in more trouble?" she said.

Eric shook his head and told her about his conversation with Lt. Mitchell. "Do you remember old Dr. Swykert, who used to visit Dad so much when we were kids?" asked Eric.

"I never liked him. He was a weird sort. I could

50

never really understand what Dad had in common with him.''

"I thought he was kind of fascinating. He reminded me of stories of mysterious old scientists busy with smoking vials of bubbling retorts in dingy laboratories, cooking up some fantastic things to startle the world.''

"That's Dr.Swykert, all right,'' said Alison. "I felt that any minute a frog would pop out of his coat pocket or a bat would fly out of his vest. He gave me the willies. I guess the only time I ever got really mad at Dad was that time he took you and me up to the old lab Swykert had at the university before he retired. Remember that?''

"No—'' Eric frowned. "Wait a minute! I do remember. How could I have forgotten a thing like that? Oh, no—''

"Oh, no, what?'' said Alison. "What's the matter with you?''

The Carlson cat pranced across the lawn, chasing a butterfly. He leaped with swift grace into the sunlight and clapped his paws together. The butterfly was quicker. The paws closed on air.

Eric watched the performance intently, waiting for the cat to repeat.

Alison shoved his arm resting on the gazebo table. "Come out of it,'' she said. "What are you dreaming about?''

Eric slowly refocused his eyes on his sister. "Alison, do you remember what happened that day Dad took us to Swykert's lab?''

"How could I forget? The old buzzard made like a doctor, saying, 'Now this isn't going to hurt one bit. Just a little pin prick is all.' Then he whacked a big slab of hide off me. I screamed bloody murder, and Dad was embarrassed. And, as I remember it, you did your share of screaming and hollering when he went at you. I'm still mad at Dad about that. Next time I talk to him, I'm going to ask why he let that old geezer do that to us."

Eric leaned across the table and stared into Alison's eyes. "Sis—can't you guess? Don't you *know* what he was doing?"

"He was weird, that's all. Touched in the head. Off his rocker. I wish you hadn't brought up his name."

"Alison—" Eric's voice was low and tense. "Did you ever hear the word, *clone?*"

Alison's face paled and her eyes widened. She was suddenly motionless, as if frozen. Her mouth opened then for a moment, and Eric thought she was going to scream. But she whispered as if suddenly seeing the incredible, the unbelievable. "No—no—it couldn't be, Eric. It couldn't be—"

Eric took her hands in his. The Carlson cat and the butterfly were still playing their deadly game. The summer air stirred.

"It *could* be," Eric said. "It could be the explanation of what we've seen. I think we've got to find Dr. Swykert—if he's still living."

When they returned to the house, Two was again absorbed in the books of Dr. Thorne's library, and Eric was glad to leave him to his reading. Eric searched among science texts to refresh his knowledge of the mysterious subject of cloning. It was simply the process of deriving one organism from another by duplication of cells. It had been done in the laboratory for a long time with simple cells. More recently, more complicated organisms had been duplicated. A mouse had been duplicated in this manner. And the dream—or the nightmare—of some scientists had been to duplicate a human being from specimens of his tissue. There were rumors of its having been done, but no proof. Eric wondered. *Did the quiet, unknown Dr. Swykert succeed in this fantastic experiment years before other scientists had seriously considered the possibility?*

Eric pointed out to Alison: "Every cell of the body contains a chromosome structure which is a blueprint for constructing others like it. Each cell contains the essence, the plan, for the whole complete structure. So it is theoretically possible to build an entire duplicate organism from a small sample of the original."

Alison was not convinced. "So if you are right, it is no longer merely theoretical. I do remember how Swykert took samples of different kinds of cells from us. From our skin. He scraped the inside of our mouths. He stuck needles into us and took deep samples. It's hard to believe Dad went along with that."

"The professor was his good friend. Dad did it as a favor; he didn't think it would hurt us in any way."

"But do you think Dad really believed Swykert would *duplicate* us?"

Eric shook his head vigorously. "I'm sure he didn't.

Dad was just humoring him for friendship's sake. And, of course, it didn't really hurt us. I had actually forgotten all about it until you reminded me."

"We'll have to call Dad," said Alison. "Something will have to be done about—*them*."

"At the right time. We have to be sure of what we're talking about. Our next move is to locate Dr. Swykert and have a chat with him."

Dr. Hamilton Swykert had been head of the department of biology and genetics at Midwest University during most of his career. Generations of students had known him first as a charming, witty instructor who could make interesting the driest of subjects. Then, later, there were those who remembered him as an increasingly difficult and irritable old man who was almost impossible to get a passing grade from; finally, only as a wisp of a figure who was rumored to be conducting forbidden experiments in the dead of night in the laboratories of the university.

He had retained his research post, but had been retired to an emeritus professorship almost twenty years before. At that time, he had gone to live in his secluded country place thirty miles beyond the outskirts of Ivy. Five years later, he had given up his laboratory at the university and had been forgotten by nearly everyone. Only Dr. Thorne and one or two other close friends who were not dead had even bothered to keep in touch with him.

Eric and Alison had difficulty in even finding where the old Swykert country place was located. They didn't want to arouse curiosity by asking. But by consulting old university directories and county recorder files, they learned where the place was located.

It was on a little-traveled road that had been superseded by a new county baseline road over a dozen years ago. Eric and Alison drove along it Tuesday morning. Eric Two had been left with his studies. He seemed quite content in Dr. Thorne's library. Aunt Rose was dubious about being left alone with Two, but Alison reassured her it was all right.

Long portions of the road were little more than a half-abandoned lane that wound alongside a canal and through rich farmland. The farms that lay adjacent to the road, however, had better access from the new baseline road.

"I'd hate to get stuck out here," said Alison. The car was bouncing at a top speed of twenty-five.

"We could build a raft and float down the canal to the main highway."

Alison slumped lower in the seat. "So build me a raft."

The day was hot, and the nearby rocky mounds radiated heat all their own. The road took a turn into low hills and wound through narrow passageways that were like walls. There were no visible tracks of other cars on the road.

"I think I see it." Eric pointed ahead.

There was a rambling structure lying atop a broad knoll. A dozen ancient trees shaded the place. As the car neared, the house appeared to Eric and Alison as if it had been built in several dissimilar sections. The most substantial was a two-story structure of red bricks that was crumbling with age. Against it was a section of stone, then other rooms of lumber, some overlaid with tarpaper with a brick pattern. Several broken windows were boarded up. Behind the house, a few sheds gave evidence that some chickens and maybe pigs and a cow or two had once belonged there. But the gates and wire sagged now. Tall weeds grew in the enclosures.

"It looks abandoned," said Alison. "I wonder whether this is the right place."

Eric stopped the car in front of a rusty, battered mailbox hanging from a post by a single loose nail. On the box were faintly visible the letters S   K  RT.

"This has to be it," said Eric.

They got out of the car and stood in front of the dilapidated place. There was complete silence except for the rustling of leaves in the giant poplar tree under which they stood.

"This is a wild goose chase," said Alison.

"Let's have a look inside. There may be clues to Swykert's work which will tell us something."

The front door was boarded up from the outside. A large weathered plank had been nailed across it long ago. The nails were rusty and loose in the wood.

"We could pull that off," said Alison.

"Let's go around first. Something may be open in back."

The ramshackle structure was actually quite large. The ground floor must contain a dozen rooms, Eric estimated, and the second-story portion was big enough to contain five or six rooms.

They came to the back, trodding down the heavy weeds as they went. Nothing was open, but the rear door was not boarded up. Eric moved aside the screen hanging from a single hinge and tried the knob. It was locked.

This door was in what appeared to be the original brick portion. A second door was located farther along in the section built of stone work. Eric moved toward it.

Behind him, Alison gave a sudden cry. "Eric!"

He whirled. She was pointing to the old-fashioned porcelain knob of the door he had just tried. It was turning slowly, twisting one way and then the other. Someone inside was attempting to open it.

Alison grasped Eric's hand and watched in hypnotic fascination the slowly turning white knob. Then, abruptly, the catch released and the door drew inward. A figure became visible in the dimness of the interior. It stepped forward into the light. A shabbily dressed young man.

His features were unmistakable.

Eric was looking once again at his own image.

# 5 • *The Laboratory*

The figure extended a hand. "Come in. I've been expecting you."

Eric and Alison felt too stunned to move.

"Who—are—you?" Alison finally gasped.

"I call myself Eric Thorne," said the young man. "Just as you do," he nodded to Eric, who eyed him closely. "We really do look much alike, don't we?" He felt his stubbled chin. "If I took a little more care about shaving and got a haircut—"

"There was another one—" said Alison.

The stranger nodded. "He left a few days ago. I should have prevented him. I suppose he created quite a stir in town, and you encountered him. That's why I expected you. You seem to have connected us with Dr. Swykert rather quickly."

"He was a friend of our father," said Eric.

"I know."

"You seem to know quite a bit about us."

58

The stranger smiled wryly again. "I should, shouldn't I—since we use the same name? Since we're practically the same person? But, please, come in. You needn't stand out there."

They passed through a hallway and entered the living room of the brick portion of the house. *This was once quite beautiful,* Eric thought. A high beamed ceiling rose overhead. A large, old-fashioned fireplace held a broken kettle bracket. The broad hearth had bricks missing.

The furniture had once been excellent, too. Now it was like a collection of second-hand junk. A faded green sofa had broken springs in one end. A scarred maple chair was on the other side next to a rickety table. The bare wooden floor was much marred.

"I don't keep a very good house," their host said. "The doctor was the same way. Never much time for such things. If you'll wait a moment, I'll call my sister to join us." He left for another room in the depths of the hallways that Eric suspected were like a rat maze.

At the mention of a sister, Alison felt a surge of anxiety again. She knew who was coming.

There were footsteps in the hall, and then she was there, framed in the doorway. The girl could have been herself in a mirror, Alison thought. Except she was so beautiful. Prettier by far than she—

The young man spoke from behind the girl. "This is—as you must have guessed—Alison. Alison, this is Eric and Alison."

The boy seemed to be enjoying the situation in a

59

twisted sort of way, but the girl's voice was edged with sadness as she said, "I'm very glad to meet you."

"You worked at Lowry's," said Alison.

The girl nodded. "I had to leave. I couldn't pass myself off as you indefinitely. So many of your old friends were there. But I wanted so much to stay. It was the first time I ever—"

Alison thought she was going to cry.

"The dresses were so pretty," the girl finally said.

The boy brought in a couple more battered chairs from the kitchen. He and Eric sat on them. The girls sat near each other on the faded sofa.

"So you met the other Eric in town?" the boy asked.

"Yes—he caused quite a stir. He's at our house now," Eric replied.

"How did you work that out—about names I mean?"

"We agreed I was Eric One, and he was Eric Two. One and Two. It was better than Social Security numbers—which he didn't have, anyway."

"Sounds good enough." The boy laughed softly. "I'll be Three, then. My sister can be Alison Two."

"But *who* are you? How—" Alison leaned forward in desperation to understand.

"Haven't you guessed?" said Three.

"Clones," said Eric.

"You've got it. You probably remember when Swykert did it."

"We were ten."

"You know about all there is to know, then," said Three. He paused and then continued. "I would much

60

rather you had never found out. It would have been better for all of us if you had never known."

"Why?" said Alison. "We've got a right to know!"

"I don't know why you should have any such right," said Three thoughtfully. "It's going to do you no good in the long run. It's only going to mean turmoil for you. Even some heartache, probably."

"Nothing you're saying makes any sense," said Alison. "Why shouldn't we know?"

Three slumped on the uncomfortable chair and looked across the room as if seeing something far distant. "Doctor Swykert was one of those rare men who had a dream and managed to keep hold of it all his life. Long before anyone heard about genetic engineering and tinkering with genes—you read about those things in the newspaper now, and stock speculators make and lose fortunes on companies who manufacture new kinds of cells in their factories—anyway, long before all that, Dr. Swykert had the dream that man could be much better than he ever had been. He set out to find a way.

"He needed people for his experiments, but he couldn't work on real people; so he decided he could make some. He'd make some copies—clones—of real people. He figured there'd be no harm in working with them. So he did it—years before any other scientists would admit it could be done. They admit it now."

"Did he use anyone else besides Alison and me?" said Eric.

"Not as far as I know. We two and the other Eric are the result. We became the first artificially produced human beings in history. Other scientists have done it with mice, but Swykert did it with us."

"Just you three?" said Alison.

"There were actually three others in the beginning. They died when they were quite young. We are the survivors."

"So where does it all lead?" asked Eric. "Where is Swykert now? What are his plans for you?"

"Swykert is dead. He was incapable of carrying on much work for the past two years. Finally, he died a month ago. We buried him on the property. He was almost ninety years old, you know."

Eric said, "You must forgive me if I seem unable to comprehend that you two are literally our "children," more so than if you had been born to us. You are *exact* copies of us. I had planned to check fingerprints. I think I would have found them identical. Am I right?"

Three nodded. "Yes. But don't be unhappy about not being able to comprehend our relationship. We understand how new this is to you, and what a shock it undoubtedly has been. For us, of course, we have known a long time. Swykert told us all about it."

"And so the three of you have to find a way to fit yourselves into a world you have never really known. I presume all of Dr. Swykert's plans for you were cancelled by his death. What *are* your plans now? And why did Two do the rather stupid things he did, robbing stores, giving us the phony story about amnesia, and all that?"

"There are some things I haven't yet told you," said

Three. "One of these is the fact that our aging process is quite different from yours. You said you remembered how cell samples were taken when you were near ten years old. Look at us: we appear to be the same age as you, maybe a little older even, yet we are actually ten years younger. We have developed and aged almost three times as fast as you."

"Sixteen years—or more—in six," said Eric uncertainly.

"And this process is accelerating—very rapidly. Today we aged a week. Soon, a day will be a month. Then— you see, our lives are going to be very short. By the end of the summer—" Three spread his hands in resignation.

Eric felt an immense sadness. He looked at Alison Two. Her eyes were glistening with tears. It was an enormous injustice that his "sons" and Alison's "daughter" would not endure long enough to find out more about the world.

"Surely something can be done," he said lamely.

"We're trying," said Three. "We're trying desperately—twenty hours a day. That's why our housekeeping and gardening isn't very good. But we don't know whether we're even on the right track. It takes hundreds and hundreds of cell experiments, and Swykert's lab is almost as much a ruin as this house."

"Maybe the university—"

"I'm sure they wouldn't go for anything connected with Swykert's research. From what he said, the current administration is quite thoroughly soured on him.

63

They remember him only as a crank. All the good things he once did are forgotten.''

"Then there's the second thing," said Three.

"Yes?"

"Eric Two. We need to persuade him to come back, if we can find him."

"I told you he's at our house right now."

"I rather doubt it," said Three. "You see, he's different from Alison Two and me. All of us have superior abilities. Swykert saw to that. But Two is far ahead of the two of us. He's like a comet blazing across the sky. Incredibly brilliant. Swykert recognized this and lavished twice as much attention on him.

"At the same time, Eric Two is an oddball, as I think you might say. He does strange things at times. Swykert knew this and kept a close leash on him. Two was loyal and devoted to Swykert and obeyed him. But Swykert is gone, and Two has taken off. I'm afraid he could get into trouble—serious trouble."

"He already has," said Eric. He described the events connected with the burglaries. "He said he needed the money for living, and that he couldn't remember where he came from—amnesia."

"He was lying to you. And he'll probably get into more mischief. That's why I say I doubt he's still at your place. With you gone, he's just as likely to go off again. I really don't know what to do with him. He could be of enormous help in our aging research, but he claimed he was working on something more important. I know he was busy here, but I don't know what he was doing. Personally, I think he's a crook—an exceedingly brilliant crook."

"But he's *me!*" Eric exclaimed. "Two is me, as much as you are!"

"He's all of us," said Three kindly. "In every man there are two sides, three sides, four sides—who knows how many? Each of us has predominant characteristics, while the rest are suppressed. How this comes about was one of the secrets Swykert was trying to solve through Two."

Alison said, "Now I *know* I don't like Dr. Swykert! I hated him that day at the university; I thought it was because I was frightened. Now I see him heartlessly experimenting on you three people as if he were working with animals."

"Just copies," said Three. His voice was without bitterness, but the kindness was gone. "We're copies, nothing more. Copies of human beings—you and Eric."

Alison Two came to life with a burst of protest. "That's not true! You know it's not true! We're as much alive as *they* are!" She thrust a hand in the direction of Eric and Alison. "We feel, we hurt, we love, we laugh, we cry—we do everything they do. Don't you understand that, Alison—Eric? We're just like you!"

She turned fiercely back to Three. "You have no right to say we aren't human. Maybe you aren't, but I am!"

She was crying.

Three watched Alison Two for a moment. Her shoulders shook with her sobbing. "Our existence has not been an easy one," he said. "Whatever we are—whoever we are—there have been difficult times. At any rate," he went on, "we should bring Two back before he gets into even more trouble."

Eric leaned his head back for a moment and let his eyes scan the ancient timbers that were the ceiling beams. He wondered who had built them. They must have been here a hundred years at least.

Clones.

It was becoming real to him that they were actually sons and daughter. He and Alison had a responsibility toward them. No matter how their creation came about, no matter how short was their span of life—regardless of these things, they were family. He and Alison had to help them. Help them find a place in the world for the short span of time left to them. Help Two straighten himself out. Teach them about God and the things Swykert hadn't told them about themselves.

Three was saying, "We'd like to have you spend the night with us. There's plenty of room. Our meals are what you would call economical. You might like to see Swykert's lab and notes and journals. I haven't read all of them myself, yet. He wrote so much, I sometimes wonder how he had time for lab work."

Eric and Alison debated the matter of staying. Aunt Rose was so used to their irregular comings and goings, it probably wouldn't upset her too much. The only real problem was Eric Two. Yet there was little they could do about that, no matter where they were. He would behave, or he would get into more trouble.

"We'd love to stay," Alison said to the clones.

They were shown rooms in the old stone section of the house by Alison Two. She apologized for the dinginess of the rooms. "I know this isn't what you're used to."

Eric looked around and wondered whether Swykert had furnished the place or whether it had always been this way from some long-forgotten owner. The decrepit washstand leaned back toward the wall. The brick under one leg, where a caster used to be, was too thick. The bed—he scarcely dared try it for fear of its collapsing. A faded patchwork cover lay on top of it. Little light made its way through the narrow, dirty window.

Alison said, "Don't worry about it. We'll be just fine. Except that if I'd known we were staying, I'd have brought my toothbrush."

Later, Eric went outside to move their car into the yard. Alison went along to get a moment alone with him. After moving the car, they watched the burning sunset from the vantage point of the rise on which the old house was located.

"What do you think?" asked Alison.

"I think we've really got our hands full. With what, I'm not sure."

"We'll have to call Dad. We can't be in Buenos Aires when he wants us to be. How much more should we tell him?"

Eric leaned against the car and looked at the unbelievable structure of the house. "Eventually, we've got to tell him everything. But we don't want him to think he's got to drop everything and come tearing home to bail us out of our problems. Yet I don't see any way not to tell him the whole story. There's no way to tell just part of it."

"He'll think we're trying to play a joke on him."

"No. He'll remember that day he took us to Swykert. In the meantime, I think we've got to move these two into town with us. They obviously need food and clothes. They can't stay out here alone with nothing to live on. Maybe we could get them some help with their research, too." *Before, the end of summer seemed a long way off,* Eric thought. *Now—*

"What about our friends and neighbors when two more of us show up around town?"

"We'll have to handle that when we get to it. I feel like I'm buried so deep now I can't see out."


Alison Two prepared dinner on an old wood range. She cooked potatoes harvested the year before from the small garden beyond the house. There was a fried chicken, which Eric suspected might have been the last inhabitant of the dilapidated hen house. They ate by the fading light of the sun and finished by candlelight.

"Swykert once had an electric generating set here," said Three. "It broke down years ago. We've been used to candles for a long time."

"It's a lovely dinner," said Alison. "You're a good cook," she said to Alison Two.

"We want you to come and live with us in town," said Eric. "Our house has plenty of room. We can provide laboratory space in our basement and maybe help out with some of your work."

"We wouldn't think of imposing on you," said Three.

"You won't be. We want to help. After all—we're *family*. Remember?"

Neither of the clones smiled at Eric's attempt at lightness. Three's face hardened, but he said nothing. Alison Two looked as if she would cry again.

After dinner, Three showed Eric and Alison the laboratory. It occupied the upstairs portion of the brick part of the house. With candle holder in hand, Three led them up a flight of creaking, unsteady steps.

What Eric had thought might be five or six upstairs rooms was one large area occupied entirely by the laboratory equipment. Most of it, however, Eric could see at once was unused. It was covered with dust and stacked in disarray on tables. Only one small area looked clean and used.

"This is where I've been working," said Three. "Swykert and I worked here as long as he was able. He was trying to find a way to identify and isolate the genes responsible for aging and alter them to prevent our premature aging. We never pinpointed what he was hoping to find. He spent twenty hours a day working here as long as he could. It wasn't enough. Since he died, Alison and I have been trying to go it alone. But we have no money for materials and equipment—and so little time."

"That's where we can help," said Eric. "We can give

you space for the equipment you need. We'll help you with the work if you'll tell us what to do. We can provide some help with materials and equipment."

Three looked around. Eric followed his glance. He wondered what kind of work they had been doing. The equipment seemed meager and in poor condition. The lab looked like little more than a run-down high-school chemistry lab.

That evening, they sat by the battered table in the living room and read by candlelight from Swykert's journals. The handwriting was difficult, and Eric found it almost impossible to follow. Even so, he caught the flavor and understood the driving power that impelled the old professor to his eccentric and lonely life.

As a young professor, Swykert had been saddened by the savagery and the insane exhilaration with which men only slightly younger than he had gone off to slaughter in the trenches of war. He determined then that men could be better than they were.

He never lost that dream.

He felt the answer lay in the stuff men were made of, in the genes that laid down the patterns by which they lived their whole lives. If that blueprint could be changed, perhaps men could devote their lives to goodness and construction instead of death and destruction.

*He missed the whole point,* thought Eric. *What about God? What about the soul—the spirit?*

"He was far, far ahead of his time in gene theory and analysis," Three said. "If he had chosen to parade his work before his colleagues in the science journals, he might have been hailed as a genius. He preferred to stick to his solitary vigil."

They read and talked until midnight, when Eric and Alison decided to go to bed. Three, however, continued to sit by the table with the journals, reading material he had not been into before.

"You go ahead," Three said. "I want to spend another couple of hours on this. With every page, I keep thinking there might be some clue that Swykert never told me about. I'll see you in the morning."

Eric and Allison said goodnight and climbed the stairs to their rooms with the aid of candles. Eric debated sleeping on the floor, but finally gave in and lay on the creaky, wobbly structure of the bed. It did not collapse. It had no springs. Only a rope, laced across the rails, supported the straw tick and the musty bedclothes. He closed his eyes and tried to sleep. It was a long time before he succeeded.

Dawn was very gray through the dust-covered windows. Eric glanced at his watch. Nearly seven. So late! He dressed quickly, wishing for his absent toothbrush and razor, and went downstairs.

With a start, he saw that Three was still sitting where he had left him. Piles of journals were on the floor. The candle had burned down, but Three was still reading by the dim light of dawn. Or, rather, had been reading.

Now, as Eric entered the room, he was holding a sheet on his lap, his eyes staring unseeingly into some far distance. He didn't stir until Eric was almost beside him.

He looked up then, his eyes wide and frightened.

Eric felt a sense of apprehension. "What is it? Is something wrong?"

Three nodded without speaking. Finally, he said, "Eric Two. I understand now why Swykert kept him on such a short leash. He shouldn't have kept him at all. He should have killed him."

"Killed him? But that would have been murder!"

Eric Three wasn't listening.

"I didn't know. There was no way I could know. Eric Two is the most dangerous man in the world. And I have turned him loose."

# 6 • Dr. Thorne's Advice

Alison Two had no eggs to serve for breakfast. She warmed potato slices and cooked oatmeal.

Three refused to talk until they were finished.

After breakfast, he led them back into the living room and took the maple chair by the table. Eric sat on a kitchen chair. The girls took the sofa. Three sat with legs crossed and papers on his knee. He didn't seem to know how to start.

"I read this last night," he said finally. "It's in Swykert's journal. Things I never knew before."

"About Two?" said Eric.

"About Two. Last night I said he was a bad apple. I just didn't know had bad. From Swykert's journals I found out how completely rotten—and dangerous—he is."

Alison remembered her own uneasy feelings when Two came to their house. "How is he bad? What will he do?"

"Swykert put it this way," said Three. " 'There are some people whose whole purpose is to destroy. The world has seen a good number of them down through the ages: the Goths, the Vikings, Napoleon, Stalin, Hitler, and a lot of lesser ones. They are psychopathic personalities.' Eric Two is one of these.

"Swykert knew it. He had identified Two's condition even when Two was a little child. He thought he knew how to save him, to show that such a person could be salvaged. As I told you, Two is intellectually brilliant. Swykert thought that brilliance could be used to turn him around. He thought sufficient knowledge, education, data would do it. He provided Two with every means of education possible. He provided books. He crammed Two's head full of data about everything on earth. Two ate it up—"

"But what about God? What about moral values?" asked Alison. "Didn't Professor—"

"Swykert never spoke of God," Three responded. "He thought of us only as machines—not humans."

"He was wrong," Eric said flatly.

For a moment there was silence. Then Eric Three seemed to collect his thoughts. "At any rate, Two absorbed all that knowledge like a sponge. His extreme genius was in the field of mathematics and electronics. On paper, he built devices and machines that would change the face of the world if they were put into use.

"And Swykert's efforts were a failure. He produced an incredible genius—who was still a psychopathic personality. Two's single emotion, according to Swykert, is rage. Rage against the world and against mankind because he is a created thing, a machine that can never be a man. His greatest invention is an EMR device—electromagnetic radiation—which can be deadly to all life forms within a vast range. Swykert believed Two's goal was to sell this device where it would be used.

"It is known the Russians have already explored the EMR concept and made some attempts at development. Within recent years, the harmful effects of ordinary, everyday radiation have been discovered in the vicinity of high-voltage power lines, near powerful antennas, even in ordinary household appliances. Two found combinations of frequencies and means of propagation that are deadly. If Swykert was right, Two is preparing to deliver his discoveries where they will be used."

Alison's voice was frightened. "If all this is true, what do you think he will do next?"

Three exhaled wearily. "What did Hitler do? What did Stalin do? The psychopath has only one purpose: destroy."

In silence, their eyes came to rest on the papers of Dr. Swykert.

"There was a story written about a hundred years ago," said Eric slowly, "about a man, a scientist, who created a human being who was a monster and turned on his inventor. The scientist's name was Dr. Frankenstein. Did you ever read the story?"

Three nodded. "Swykert had it in his library. He *seemed* to read it frequently. But he never understood its warning."

They fell silent again, and in the silence, there grew the faint sound of a car. Eric turned his head about and listened intently. "Does anyone else ever drive along this road?"

"No. Never—" Three went to the dust-covered window and tried to peer out. Nothing was visible from that point. The sound grew louder.

Three raced up the stairway. His footsteps were heard from the upper level as he moved from window to window. There was a moment of silence. Then his hurrying footsteps were heard from the stairs again.

"It's Two!" he exclaimed. "Two is coming back!"

Eric jumped up to try to see from the window. "How can he? He has no car."

"He's got Swykert's old car. It hadn't run for five years, but somehow he got it going. That's just a sample of his talent."

"Another is the fact that Sheriff Rayburn confiscated that car in Midland. How did Two get it back again?"

They waited, listening to the sound of the aged, slow-moving vehicle. "Do you have any idea what to expect?" said Eric. "Will he be violent or hostile toward you—and us?"

"I have no way of knowing. He disliked me and Alison because we didn't share his feelings. But I don't know why he's come back or what to expect of him."

"Do you have a gun?"

"No. Nothing."

"If he's hostile, he could be armed," said Eric. "He could have obtained a gun when he recovered his car."

Through the window, they glimpsed the old green car come to a stop in front of the house. Two got out quickly and moved toward the house. He disappeared around the corner. They faced the rear of the room as Two rammed open the back door carelessly and strode in.

He grinned with an arrogance that Eric had not seen before. Two had been a very good actor in their previous encounters.

"Hello, everybody," he said.

Eric smiled. "Hello, Two. We didn't expect you to follow us. We thought you would be happy at our place."

"It became boring after you left. I read all the books in your library, and there was nothing much left to do. I told your aunt I was going to look for you. She was getting worried when you didn't show up last night."

"That was thoughtful of you."

Alison Two said, "Have you had breakfast? I'll fix something for you if you're hungry."

Two laughed softly. "That's very sisterly of you. But no, I didn't come for breakfast. I just stopped by for one important thing."

"What's that?" asked Three.

"The journals and records—all those books that Swykert kept about us. I want you to bring them down here. I see you've been looking at some of them this morning. Bring them all, every one of them. I know how many there are because I saw him pouring over them enough times. Don't try to hold any back."

Three looked at him steadily. "I don't think I want to do that."

Two returned his gaze. "I think you do." A gun appeared in his hand. "The rest of you stay over there by the front window while Eric—what do they call you? I'll bet it's Three. It is, isn't it?" He laughed without humor. "Get moving, Three. I know how to use this gun, and it's loaded."

"I'll help," said Eric.

"You stay where you are. Three can do the job very nicely by himself."

For twenty minutes Eric and the two girls watched silently as Three went up and down the stairs bringing the thick loose-leaf notebooks down to the living room and piling them on the floor.

Only once was the silence broken. Two said to Three, "Don't do that."

"Don't do what?"

"Don't chuck some of the books through the upstairs window onto the roof. I *know* how many there should be. Bring them all."

While the pile had grown high, Eric Two turned to Alison and her clone daughter. "I want you girls to start a fire in the fireplace. There are matches on the mantle."

"What do we use for wood?" said Alison.

"These." Two kicked the pile of journals. "Tear out the pages. See that they are all burned very carefully. I don't want any pages left."

From the stairway came Three's anguished cry. "No!

You can't burn the journals. It's his only record. It's all of Dr. Swykert's life work!''

"Yes, isn't it," said Two. "And I don't want any of it left. Don't try to stop me!" He brandished the gun threateningly. "It might be wisest for me to kill you all, but with the records gone, nothing you could say would matter very much. Get busy! Burn those pages!"

One by one, handful by handful, the irreplacable records went up in bursting, yellow flames. The room grew oppressive with the heat. They continued watching until the last page crinkled and turned black.

Three was almost sobbing. "Why did you have to do that? You monster! All that work destroyed!"

"All that the journals told about me is gone, too," said Two. "I'm about to start on the career for which the good doctor prepared me. I couldn't have that information about my origin still in existence, could I?"

"What career are you talking about?" demanded Alison.

"The only career for which clones are naturally prepared. My brother and sister clones don't understand that, but then there are imperfections in clones as well as men."

"We don't understand, either," said Alison. "What is this great career of yours?"

"You *wouldn't* understand," said Two in fury and bitterness. "You can't possibly know what it is like to look like a man—or a woman—and not be one, can you? That is I! That's all of us!" He swept an arm toward the other clones. "I walk and talk like a man, but I can never be one. I'm a thing. I was made by a man, a thing to be manipulated and experimented upon.''

"You are a man,'' Eric said quietly. "You're as human as I am. You have the same body as I, even down to the fingerprints. Your thoughts and your feelings—''

"You'd like me to believe that, wouldn't you? So would I! But it's not true. I'm only your shadow, and when the light comes up, shadows cease to exist. If I *could* be human, I'd laugh and run and cry out with all the joy in the world. But there's no joy for a shadow.''

"I'll show you,'' said Eric. "I'll help you.''

"No. There's nothing to show—except what I'm going to show *you*. I'm going to tear down your world. That's my career. It's the only career for a clone. I'm going to rip apart this world of men who mock me and have made me a *thing*. When I'm through, there will be no men left. And the shadows will be gone, too—

"It's all so easy, you know. Men hate each other so much that only a small trigger is needed to set them at each others' throats. Only a single, small trigger, and they will instruct their hired technicians to ignite the rockets and drown the world in atomic fire. And I can set off that small trigger!''

They huddled together at the side of the fireplace as if his words were stones hurled by a madman. He grinned at them. "Isn't that a thought? Isn't that a tremendous thought?''

He stared and grinned insanely for a long minute.

Then he whirled and darted out the back door. In a moment, from the side of the house, there were two shots.

"Our tires," said Eric. "He shot our tires so we couldn't follow."

The girls clung to each other. Three just stared at the charred remains of the pages in the fireplace, a few still glowing.

"Our work on the anti-aging research was in there," said Alison Two.

"Get your things," said Eric. "Clothes, personal effects. We'll come back for other stuff later. We'll drive the car on the rims until we get to town."

No one argued or offered suggestions. It seemed the only thing to do.

They took over five hours of tense, slow, jolting driving to reach the first garage on the main road. Fortunately, extra wheels and tires to fit Eric's car were available there. He called Lt. Mitchell while repairs were being made.

"Lt. Mitchell? Eric Thorne. You win," he said in a tired voice. "That guy that looked like me. He's gone. He's got a gun and threatened us with it. He's in the green car that he somehow got back from Sheriff Rayburn. I'd suggest you get out a statewide alert for him. He's very dangerous."

Ed Mitchell said thanks and hung up. *He'll save his I-told-you-so's until later,* Eric thought.

"Dad's next," Eric said to Alison. "Have you figured out how we're going to put it to him?"

She shook her head. "I haven't got any ideas about

anything. I feel numb all over, especially between the ears."

Eric shook her by the arm. "Come on, Sis. This is probably the most serious thing we've ever faced."

"I know. I'm sorry, Eric. I've just never been so scared in all my life. And yet—" she hesitated, "I almost feel sorry for him. Did you hear what he said? He's only a thing, a shadow of a human being. That's not true, is it? I know it isn't. These clones are as real as you or I. If only he could be made to understand that, maybe he wouldn't be the way he is."

"But he doesn't understand it, and he's out to trigger World War III. With his genius, he can do it. We've got to get to him first."

They reached home by dark. Alison realized they wouldn't have to explain Three to Aunt Rose. She would go on thinking he was Two. Alison Two was a new problem, however.

Alison entered the house first by the rear door. The housekeeper was preparing dinner, assuming they would be home.

"Here we are!" announced Alison. Then she knew Aunt Rose had caught sight of Alison Two by the way the housekeeper's jaw dropped and her eyes widened. But before she could utter her exclamation of disbelief Alison said quickly. "Aunt Rose, I know you won't believe this, but—"

"I don't want to hear it!" she interrupted. "I just don't want to hear it!" Alison's explanation of Eric Two had been all she could bear.

"Get washed up and I'll put some more stretcher in the chili so I can feed you all. You've got ten minutes!"

Eric and Alison hurried their guests upstairs and showed them their rooms. When Alison saw what clothes their guests had brought, she hastily told Eric they would have to give up some of their own. The clones only had worn jeans and badly patched shirts. Eric got out some more of his, thinking of what he had already given Two, which had disappeared. "I'm not going to have anything left," he said in mock disgust.

Alison shushed him while she got some spare slacks and blouses of her own for Alison Two.

The clones looked very presentable when they came downstairs for dinner.

The meal went well. There was little they could say to each other, but Aunt Rose kept up a running account of the robbery of Mr. Barrett's store. "He's such a nice man, a friend to everybody in town. You can't imagine anybody doing a thing like that to him."

Eric listened to her rambling words. He wondered whether the story was out that the burglar was a dead ringer for Eric Thorne. Evidently it wasn't. For that, he was glad.

After dinner, Eric and Alison showed their guests the library, which had been put back in order after Two had taken half the books off the shelves. Three looked at the titles, at the science, the history, the geography materials.

"It's too bad he got hold of these. This information will help him—in what he plans to do."

"He couldn't absorb all that in the time he was here," Eric said.

"But he could. It's very easy—"

Alison's eyes widened. "You, too?"

Three nodded. "That was one of Dr. Swykert's gifts. He didn't leave us many. But that was one."

"You must have others," said Eric. "Your I.Q.—"

"High enough. But that means little when you're— like us."

Alison snapped, almost angrily. "What do you mean: like us? You sound like Two. You're no different than Eric and I."

"I wish that were true."

But Alison Two grasped at the reassurance. "Do you really believe it, Alison? Do you really think it's possible?"

Alison put an arm about her new-found daughter. "Of course, I'm sure."

The clones wanted to explore the library. Eric and Alison let them browse through the books while they went up to Eric's bedroom to put in a call to their father. There was an extension for each of them. It was a private line with special security circuits.

It took a while for Dr. Thorne to be located, but he finally came on. It was mid-afternoon of a hot, muggy day where he was.

"Hello—who is this? Eric! How are you? It's good to hear your voice."

"Hi, Dad," added Alison.

"Hello, Alison. So what's up?"

Eric stumbled for words he suddenly didn't know how to choose. "There's something, Dad—I just don't know where to start."

"Try the beginning." Dr. Thorne sounded in good humor.

"The beginning? Well, I guess it starts that day you took Alison and me to visit your old friend at the university when we were about ten. Do you remember that?"

"What old friend? I was always taking you with me to visit people."

"Yeah, well, this particular time, Dr. Swykert."

"Who? Oh, yes—old Swykert! Yes, he must have died a long time ago. I haven't been in touch with him for quite a while."

"He died just recently."

"I see. Well, he must have been a very old codger, then. But you didn't call just to tell me Swykert was dead."

Eric swallowed hard and looked at Alison as if for help. "Do you remember what Swykert did? He took tissue samples from Alison and me. He scraped our skin and mouth tissues. He punched a few needles in us, and he—"

"Oh, yes—I remember now. I was always sorry about that. I never told you, I guess, but I regretted it. Old Swykert assured me it would be painless and harmless, but I could see it wasn't after we got there. He wanted a few samples of live human cells for some experiments he was doing, and I agreed just to humor him.

He was getting a little dotty even then. Nothing ever came of it, of course."

"Something *did* come of it, Dad. Have you ever heard of clones?"

There was suddenly an immense silence on the line except for the occasional scratch and hiss of the circuits. Eric thought he had been disconnected for a moment.

Then his father's voice came as if from a great distance. *"Clones?* Eric—what are you talking about?"

"You know what clones are, Dad?"

"Of course, I know. Swykert babbled about it several times in his ridiculous little laboratory. Crackpot biologists have been talking about it ever since they found out how to transfer genes from one cell to another. They even talk of human clones—the idiots!"

"No, Dad," Eric said softly. "It's for real. Swykert did it. He cloned *us*—Alison and me. There are two clones of me and one of Alison."

There was a moment of silence on the line again until Dr. Thorne said flatly, "I don't believe it, Eric. It's an utter impossibility. And certainly that wild-eyed Swykert could never have accomplished it. Tell me what's going on there."

Eric told the story, beginning with the visit of Lt. Mitchell and ending at the present moment with Three and Alison Two in the house.

Eric sensed the distress in his father's voice when Dr. Thorne spoke again. But his father was insistent. "I tell you it's impossible, Eric! These—whoever they are—

can't possibly be duplicates of you and Alison. You're letting your imagination run away with you."

"Would you believe fingerprints, Dad? They're identical."

"That's one thing that *is* impossible. I know something about fingerprint identification, and I assure you that even though there may be deceiving similarities, there will be differences."

"If you could only see us together—"

"Is there something you need me urgently for? If there is—if you need my help—I'll be on the next plane. This job is important, but I'll drop it if I have to."

Eric wished immensely that his father were there. He glanced at Alison, holding the other phone. She nodded her head slowly.

"I guess we need some kind of help, Dad. You see, the clone Two, we call him, is—well, I guess he's insane. He's got it in for the whole world because of what he is, and he swears he's going to wipe it out. He says he can do it by setting nations at each other's throats."

"He sounds like a typical crackpot," said Dr. Thorne. "The police ought to be able to handle him."

"You don't understand, Dad. His I.Q.—and that of the other clones—is way up in the 200 range. Two is the most brilliant genius of all—and as insane as Hitler or Stalin ever were. He's got to be stopped!"

Dr. Thorne cleared his throat. "That does sound serious. Are the other two people giving you any problem?"

"No. We're becoming good friends with them."

"I think what I should do is get in touch with the CIA and have them send one of their best men out to take care of this Two, as you call him. An experienced agent could certainly do far more in this instance than I could, even if I were there. After you've talked with the man, call me again. Then, if there's any need, I'll come. O.K.?"

"That's great," said Eric. He felt relieved of part of the load, at least. "We wouldn't want you here need-lesssly. I'm sure the CIA can give us the help we need, if you can get them on it."

"I can. Goodbye, Eric—Alison."

"Goodbye, Dad," they said together.

"And Eric—just don't say anything about clones."

They heard the line go dead. Eric and Alison replaced the phones and looked at each other in silence.

# 7 • *Jim Holcomb*

Eric and Alison went downstairs. The two clones were still reading eagerly. Eric and Alison sat down, and Eric related their father's comments.

Three frowned as he finished. "What's this CIA? I haven't read about that."

"It's a government organization devoted to gathering intelligence about potential enemies. It also counters the efforts of those potential enemies to spy on us. Both sides play pretty rough games."

Three cupped his chin and looked at Eric thoughtfully. "Two would search out the enemy spy channels for his own purposes, wouldn't he?"

"He'd have to know how to do it. It would be risky. Alison and I have brushed with them a time or two. They aren't the kind of people you'd invite to your house to have dinner."

"Two would give them his EMR secrets," said Three. "Then he would spread information—false, of

91

course—that one group was arming against another and planning an attack."

"They aren't dummies," said Eric. "They're used to playing that kind of game. They can spot the real from the phony. Two would likely find himself thrown from a car on some lonely road in an Arabian desert—with bullets in him. Amateurs can't play with the professionals in that league."

"I think he will try," said Three with conviction.

Eric shifted his thoughts. "It's strange he hasn't been picked up already by the local police. They have a pretty tight network. If he's still traveling in that green car, he's sure to be nailed."

Three shook his head emphatically. "He's smarter than that. I think he's still in town. He won't try to get out in that car. I've got an idea he just might try to float with a piece of driftwood along that stream I saw that flows south out of town. We crossed it on the way in."

"Hey! I wonder if Lt. Mitchell has thought of that. He could mount some lights on the highway bridge over the creek. Nothing could get past."

"Do you think Two would float down if he saw those lights there?"

"Yeah, I guess you're right."

"Call the lieutenant in the morning and suggest he comb the area below the bridge very carefully in the daylight. He might have some luck."

"If he does, we won't need any CIA help."

"Right. We wouldn't need them at all."

It sounded good. But Eric had the feeling Three did

not believe it. The clone kneaded his fingers nervously. Then he stood up.

"I wonder whether it would be all right if I went out for a little walk in the dark," he said. "I'd like to stretch my legs a bit. Nobody would be likely to recognize me if I kept to the unlighted streets. If they did, I guess it wouldn't hurt if I just said hello and hurried on, would it?"

Eric frowned. He hated to run the risk of complicating the situation any further. But he realized how Three must feel. "Why don't we all go for a little stroll?"

"I'd sort of like to be alone," said Three. "It's been a rough day—"

"Sure. I understand. All right, then. Just don't get lost. Let me give you a flashlight to use if you need it."

When the door had closed on Three, Alison turned to Alison Two, "How about you? Are you getting jumpy, too?"

Alison Two smiled and shook her head. "No. I'm just glad to be here. It's so pleasant to be in a real house. We've never lived in one, you know. We never knew anything but that shack of Dr. Swykert's. He was kind to us, but he had no idea what a house should be. The place was always jammed to the ceiling with his work materials that no one else was allowed to touch. I wish I could stay here with you forever!"

"You can stay here as long as you like," said Alison.

"Till the end of summer?"

For a moment Alison and Eric failed to understand her meaning. Then they remembered.

"Surely there's more time than that," said Eric gently.

"No. That will be all, if that. I thought for a while there might be some hope when Three and Dr. Swykert were working together on their aging research. But now that's gone, all their work destroyed in the fire today. Besides, Three has no more interest in it. He feels nothing is of any importance to us except destroying Two."

"I thought he planned to set up a laboratory in our basement," said Alison.

"He sees no use of doing so, with our notes gone, and the urgency of capturing Two. In a month or two— There's just no time. No time."

Alison Two excused herself to go upstairs to bed.

Eric watched her go. *The research ought to be the main goal,* he thought, *not the pursuit of insane Two. Surely it shouldn't be such a problem to capture one lone criminal fleeing from a place like Ivy. If Lt. Mitchell could just put enough good men on the job—if the State Highway Patrol would concentrate on it—*

*The trouble is that they don't know the urgency. They think they're after a two-bit burglar who robbed a supermarket. It isn't a big deal. It won't matter that much whether they catch him or not.*

*It's not as if the fate of the world might be at stake.*

*Not to them, anyway.*

Maybe he should have explained all this to Ed Mitchell, he thought. But that would have been futile. The lieutenant was a good, honest, likable, hard-working man. But the concept of clones was as far beyond his capacity to understand as little green men from Mars.

*After all,* Eric thought, *if Dad put it down as my wild imaginings, who would believe?*

The CIA?

Quite unlikely. Dr. Thorne had said not to mention clones to the agent. But how could he tell the story without it?

The workaday world of the CIA is not the fictional one of the James Bonds and George Smileys. Eric and Alison had had small contacts with their agents in the past and learned to respect them as hard working men and women in a sometimes dangerous profession, but no more so than that of a New York City policeman.

As with people everywhere, some in the CIA were dull and unimaginative clockwatchers; others were conscientious, and they saw their jobs contributing to the stability of an already too-shaky world. Still others had the vision and imagination to detect villainy where no one else could see it, and pursue it to the bitter end at whatever cost to themselves.

There were only a handful of these. The chance that one of them would be assigned to a weird-sounding case in the obscure town of Ivy was very remote.

"I guess I'll go to bed, too," said Alison. "Are you going to wait up for Three?"

"I'd better." He glanced at the clock. "I shouldn't have let him go. He's been gone too long now. If anything happens to him, things will be infinitely worse."

It was eleven o'clock. Eric Three had been gone since nine-thirty. Eric went out to the front porch, berating himself for letting Three go. He sat on the top step to wait. The night was dark and moonless. A street light far down on the next corner gave the only illumination except for a few lighted windows up and down the street.

More than a half hour later, Eric was still sitting there. But he began to hear a faint sound from somewhere down the street, a kind of shuffling, as if someone were walking very slowly and perhaps painfully. Eric strained his eyes to see into the darkness. Strangers were few on the streets of Ivy this time of night. It *could* be Three. Had he hurt himself in the darkness?

Eric went to the front gate, keeping to the darkest shadows. The outline of the walker began to appear against the distant glow of the street lamp.

It was the clone, and he was limping.

Eric opened the gate and ran down the street toward him. "What happened to you? Are you hurt? You're all wet!"

The clone stopped. He turned a bit, and the glow of the street lamp caught his face. He was grinning sheepishly.

"I fell in," he said.

"Fell in what?"

"The creek. I went down by the creek and walked along the bank just to get an idea of what it might be like if Two tried to escape that way. I slipped and fell into the water. I scraped my knee on a rock and twisted

96

my ankle. I guess I really botched up my first attempt to explore Ivy!"

Eric felt a surge of anger for letting Three go, but he kept his voice calm.

"It's O.K. No harm done. But let's get you in the house and clean you up and see what first aid you need."

"I'm sorry, Eric." He sounded deeply remorseful for his goof. "I lost the flashlight, too."

"No problem."

Eric's dismay passed. He was glad to have the clone back. He led him through the back door into the kitchen to avoid Aunt Rose's ire if she found mud tracked through the front of the house.

"Stand on this newspaper," said Eric. "Take off those wet things. I'll get a bathrobe, and you can go upstairs and take a shower."

When Eric returned with the robe, the clone had dropped the muddy clothes in a pile. A long red slash showed where he had slid his left leg against a rock. There was a bruise on his chest, too. A deep gash on his right arm was still bleeding.

"I hadn't noticed that." He held up the arm as if it didn't even belong to him.

"It looks like you smashed your face into a tree limb or something, too. Boy, you really did it up right!" He extended the robe. "Put this on and get yourself a shower while I hunt up the first aid kit."

Eric's look-alike limped away toward the hall. Eric said, "You must have lost your wrist watch, too."

The clone paused and looked at his left wrist in dismay. "I hadn't noticed. I'm sorry that's gone. Dr. Swykert gave me that a long time ago. I wanted to remember him." With a look of sadness at his bare wrist, he resumed his limping walk toward the stairs.

Eric gathered up the wet clothes. The pants and shirt were covered with white clay. Eric knew where that had come from. There was only one place on the creek bank where the white clay was exposed. It was down by the planing mill south of town. A long way—nearly three miles. He wondered why the clone had gone so far in the dark. Had he supposed he really knew where Two might be found?

Eric put the wet, muddy clothes in the basement washroom. Aunt Rose would raise a fuss over them. He cleaned up the kitchen floor and went upstairs.

The clone was waiting in his room.

"You sure took a long walk," said Eric.

"It was a stupid idea," the clone admitted. "I had kind of an idea I might be able to locate Two along the creek somewhere. No chance, of course, in the dark like that, even if he had been there. But I thought it was worth a try. I was just about to turn back when I slipped and fell into the water."

Eric applied antispetic salve to the long abrasion on his double's leg. "What do you think he's done?"

"He probably slipped out earlier this evening. I noticed little boats and scows along the bank. He could easily have taken one of those, gone beyond town, and then hitched a ride down the highway."

"That would mean he's abandoned the green car somewhere. I wonder whether it's been found yet."

"Right. He had no further need of it. He'll steal what he needs—he'll be careful now; he's learned the ropes of burglarizing. Then he'll probably move on to Canada, Europe, the Middle East—he'll find a way to get a passport—and there's where he'll try to create his international upsets."

"That's the way you'd do it?" said Eric.

The clone smiled grimly. "That's the way I'd do it."

"Then that's where we'll have to follow him. It's crazy to think that if we'd only stopped him right here in Ivy—"

"A few minutes ahead of us is as good as ten thousand miles."

At breakfast the next morning, they sat together at the small table that Elizabeth Thorne had first painted green, then red with flowered appliques, then green again, which it now was, lighter than the first green.

The two clones regarded the beautifully done eggs and crisp bacon and toast and milk as if they had never seen such fare—which they may not have, Eric supposed. They ate as if every mouthful were an incredible delight.

Alison Two gazed out at the rose garden. "So beautiful—" she said, "I never knew such flowers existed."

"Our mother planted them," said Alison. "She had a very green thumb."

"Green thumb?" Alison Two looked puzzled.

Alison laughed and explained. Then Alison Two laughed with her in understanding. Suddenly she pointed beyond the window. "What's that?"

She was pointing toward the Carlson's cat making his morning round of the rose garden.

"Just the neighbor's cat," said Alison. "He hangs around here every morning and goes home to sleep the rest of the day."

Alison Two stared at the graceful little animal in amazement. "I never saw one before."

They were suddenly aware of Aunt Rose's sharp interest in their conversation. Alison Two added hastily, "I mean, I never saw a cat just like that. Such pretty stripes—"

Out of the corner of her eye, Alison saw Aunt Rose turn back to her stove. Alison said, "There probably never was a cat—just like that."

They were scarcely finished with breakfast when the doorbell rang. Eric answered and almost closed it with a we-don't-want-any-today. It was early for vacuum cleaner salesmen.

But the stranger already had his wallet out. There was a card with a long list of information on it, but all Eric remembered were the large, significant letters CIA. He looked up at the man. The stranger was smiling and adjusting his horn-rimmed spectacles like an enthusiastic high-school science teacher.

"I'm Jim Holcomb," he said. "I was instructed to call at this address. Do you have a message for me?"

"We certainly do. Come on in."

Eric looked at him closely as the man came through the doorway. *Not more than thirty,* Eric thought. *Maybe less. Probably the greenest man in the office. He'll never believe our story. He'll never do us any good.*

Eric introduced him to the group. "You'll notice," he said, "that we resemble each other rather closely, rather like a set of quadruplets." He wanted to get that out of the way immediately.

Jim Holcomb nodded, still smiling, as if he found nothing unusual in this fact.

"My name is Eric, and this is my twin sister, Alison. *This* girl, who looks like Alison has the same name, so we call her Alison Two."

Jim Holcomb nodded again. "Quite sensible," he said.

"And this fellow, who looks like me, just happens to be Eric, also. There is a third boy, who isn't here. Since he has the same name as we do, he is called Eric Two, and this boy here is called Eric Three."

Jim Holcomb shook hands all around. "I'd say you have worked out a rather confusing situation very ingeniously." He sat down in the chair Eric offered. "Now," he said. "There was a message in our office yesterday that came in through channels from a Dr. Thorne, who is, I believe, the father of you folks."

"Yes," said Eric. "We'll explain more about this in a minute."

"Good. You might like to know that I am rather well acquainted with your father. I don't know whether he may have told you. I was on assignment in Zambeze a couple of years ago, and our paths crossed there. We were able to offer each other some mutual assistance. I have had a great admiration for Dr. Thorne ever since. I like to think he requested my assistance now because he returns that regard."

"He never mentioned it," said Eric. He began to view the agent in a new light. If he was a friend of their father—

"Tell me about it," said Jim Holcomb. He settled back in his chair expectantly.

Eric did. He began with Lt. Mitchell's visit and ended with Three's falling into the creek last night. Holcomb said nothing as the story unwound. The pleasant smile never left his face.

"That's all," said Eric finally.

"That's quite a story," said Holcomb. He glanced speculatively at the two doubles. "Clones," he said. "Very remarkable."

Alison Two burst out. "Stop looking at us like that! We're not freaks. We're as human as any of the rest of you!"

Jim Holcomb remained unmoved. "I'm terribly sorry if my glance was misinterpreted. All I see are two very lovely and handsome young people."

Alison Two bit her lips and looked down at her hands. "I'm sorry, too. I apologize."

"No need," said Holcomb.

"It's a difficult relationship," said Alison. "None of us has become quite used to it yet."

"I can understand. But that is not the problem with which you wished my help, of course. You are concerned about the threats and irrationalities of Two."

"Very much so," said Eric. "We're convinced he has an incredible weapon he intends to give other countries to use against each other and against us. He has the genius to create explosive international situations—and intends to do so. We think he must be stopped—for the safety of the whole world."

"He slipped through our hands yesterday," said Alison. "If we had been able to hold him, none of this would have been necessary."

Holcomb smiled again. "And how would you have held him? Had him jailed for a few weeks for burglary and then turned loose again?"

"That might have been enough," said Eric, "considering the aging problem I told you about." He avoided looking at the clones.

"I was forgetting that. It is an important factor. It means he's got to work fast. And we've got to work even faster."

# 8 • *The Hunt Begins*

Lieutenant Mitchell called at that moment to tell Eric the old green car had been found. It was abandoned not far from the spot where the clone said he fell into the creek. It was being brought down to the police station.

"Could you let us take a look at it?" said Eric. "I've got a friend here who's interested and would like to come with me."

Ed Mitchell grumbled a little. "It's kind of irregular; this could be evidence. But then it's no big deal, I guess. Bring your friend and come on down."

Jim Holcomb wanted to see everything. But he desired his identity kept secret for the time being. He and Eric went alone to the station to look at the car. Lt. Mitchell acknowledged Eric's introduction and went out with them to the car.

Holcomb simply looked. He took no pictures. He looked at the interior, on the floor, the seats, the trunk, the glove compartment. His eyes scanned the weathered and dented body. He looked under the hood. Satisfied at last, he wiped his hands and smiled.

"Want to make an offer?" Lt. Mitchell asked with sarcasm at his detailed inspection. "When we get through with it as evidence, we'll probably put it up for sale."

"I wouldn't mind having it as a souvenir," said Jim Holcomb.

Back in Eric's car, Jim Holcomb said, "Now I'd like to see the creek area where Three went last night thinking he might run into Two, and fell in." For this, they returned to the house and picked up the clone.

Eric knew the area, opposite the planing mill. He drove the last mile along the creek road that ran parallel a hundred yards from the stream.

The clone pointed to a path that took off from the road toward the creek. "I went that way," he said.

They parked the car and walked along the narrow path, used mostly by children playing and fishing along the creek bank. They passed through patches of thick brush that stuck to their clothes, then a cluster of trees growing in isolation along the bank. In the midst of the grove, they stood above the exposed bank of white clay.

"That's where I slipped."

Holcomb nodded, scarcely pausing. His eyes scanned the broken brush and the slick spot that looked like a place where someone had slid into the water.

"This is as far as I went," said the clone.

Holcomb stopped and turned around, still scanning

the terrain. "I guess there wasn't much to see here in the dark," he said.

"I didn't expect to see much. It was just kind of an idea I had. Not a very sensible one, really."

"But you think Two really could have got away by floating down the creek?"

"I feel almost certain that is the way he would have gone—probably only two or three hours ahead of our looking for him."

They drove next to Swykert's old place. Three had locked it, although there was nothing to lock it against. "I guess I lost the key along with my flashlight and watch," the clone said. "It wasn't in my pocket when I took the wet pants off last night. I'm sure it was there earlier."

"No matter," said Holcomb. "I presume it won't matter to force our way?"

Without waiting for an answer, he leaned against the door. It seemed to Eric that he put no effort into it at all, but the door burst open, the jamb hanging from splinters of wood.

"You lead the way," Holcomb said to the clone.

He showed the agent the living room—and the ashes that remained of Swykert's notes—the kitchen, the bedrooms, the upstairs laboratory.

Here, Eric's heart sank. Seeing again the decrepit laboratory in which such a great miracle was supposed to have been performed, it looked worse than before. Nothing could have come out of such a rathole as this.

"It was not always this way," the clone was saying.

"When I was a child, it was a place of fantastic wonder. Everything was clean; the glassware and equipment were spotless. Everything just so. Swykert was precise. He was a skillful technician. That electron microscope—" He pointed to a dust-covered instrument, long neglected. "That was his pride and joy."

"But here—" he went over to the other side of the room and lifted a large plastic cover from a cluster of six egg-shaped objects that Eric had not been aware of before. "These," he said with a kind of obvious reverence, "were the heart of all his work."

"What are they?" said Holcomb.

"These are the places where we—we clones—grew from tiny clusters of cells to mature, living, breathing infants. These vesssels were our mothers, so to speak. In here, we rested on plastic cushions surrounded by the tissue that Swykert had prepared to feed us and nourish us through the first nine months of our lives. In here were circulated the nutrients that fed us and the fluids that carried away the wastes of our bodies. This one—" He tapped one of the dusty shells—"this one is where I lay. That one over there was Alison's. And this—this was Two's."

There was a moment of awed silence as Eric and Holcomb looked upon these vessels. It was overwhelming to contemplate the miracle that had taken place in them.

Holcomb broke the spell. "He must have had a good source of funds for such elaborate and expensive equipment."

"I don't know. We often ate little more than bread and milk—sometimes without the milk. We baked the bread ourselves, Alison and I. He spoke of 'war surplus' materials. I didn't know what that meant."

Holcomb shook his head. "Even so, there are many thousands of dollars worth of equipment here. If I'm not mistaken, that's a mass spectrometer on that table over there."

Eric had not realized the laboratory wealth that lay under the dirt and chaos. He looked at Holcomb again. The agent had recognized the complex instrument, the mass spectrometer. What kind of background knowledge did the man really have?

Holcomb poked about at length. Finally, he seemed satisfied with his inspection. "This material ought to be preserved. It certainly should not be left abandoned here. The university ought to be interested if Swykert left no heirs."

"His only heirs are his clones," said Eric.

"And we have no interest in it—not any more." The clone's voice was more bitter than Eric had heard before.

They returned to the house. The girls joined them, and they congregated in the living room. The rest waited for Jim Holcomb to speak. To Eric, he seemed a little less like a high-school science teacher. He seemed older and more mature.

"You are wondering what I am going to say," he began slowly. "You are wondering whether I'm going to tell you I don't believe a word of what you've told

110

me. Am I going to say that clones are an impossibility, and this is the craziest nonsense I ever heard?"

Eric stared at him, wondering where Holcomb was going. If he should turn his back on them now—

"That's what some of my colleagues would tell you. Most of them, in fact. There's no evidence whatever to support the claim that you are clones. Nothing but the rather strange circumstances of some unusual look-alikes, and a mysterious laboratory that evidently belonged to an eccentric old professor."

"Fingerprints—" Eric muttered hoarsely.

"That would be a little difficult, but there are those who would brush them off." He smiled and looked around the group. "It's fortunate for you I was called in on this case. I don't know of anyone else who wouldn't have thrown up his hands and called it nonsense. I'm not going to do that."

The others relaxed their intolerable tension and sighed in relief.

"What are you going to do?" said Alison.

"A proper scientific evaluation is needed," said Holcomb. "Studies should be made to find out what Swykert knew—data that would evidently have been readily available if his papers hadn't been destroyed.

"But that brings us to the criminal element: Eric Two. Obviously this has to have priority. I believe you are telling the truth when you say he has the intelligence and determination to upset world affairs. I am convinced we must find him and neutralize him."

"While that's going on, couldn't something be done

for the clones, who are aging so terribly fast?" asked Eric.

Holcomb pressed his fingers together. "I said that I believe you. I didn't say that it would be easy to get anyone else to believe. In fact, I know it would be almost impossible to get any respected scientist to say that he believes your story. It would take a matter of years to bring it to the proper attention of the scientific community."

"Why do you believe us if you think no one else would?" asked Alison. "Couldn't the same evidence—"

Holcomb smiled thinly. "I take pride in having developed a special talent. Scientists don't have it—they wouldn't want it. But I have it. I can *smell* a lie. Some few of us get that way in this business, where we deal with lies and deceptions constantly. You are not lying."

"We can't just let them die while we do nothing!" Alison protested.

"I can take care of the criminal problem. About the other, I can do nothing. I cannot even allow my mind to dwell on it. I'm sorry."

Eric's double broke the sudden silence. "We understand. I think no one but ourselves could solve that problem, and we have no time. Do not concern yourself, Mr. Holcomb. It is our affair, and we are at peace."

"Thank you." Holcomb shifted in his chair as if to turn his mind to other things. "Three," he said, looking directly at the clone, "if you were in the shoes of your

112

brother clone, Two, what would you have done after escaping from here?"

"Head for the Middle East, Arabia. That's the location of the world's greatest tension at present. A very small miscalculation there could send the world up in flames."

Holcomb nodded. "I agree. That is where we will go. I will be in touch with you very soon. You two men will accompany me. The girls will remain."

Alison stormed in protest that night. "I'm not going to sit here while you go fooling around in the undercover world of Arabia! You and I have always been together in these things. We're not going to split up now!"

Eric waved his arms in resignation. "Look, Sis, I'm not making the rules. Besides, it makes sense. We can't have a whole parade going over to Arabia looking for Two while he's trying to make foreign agent contacts. Three is needed, and I'm needed—"

"And I'm not?"

"You're needed here," said Eric gently. "There's Alison Two. She needs you. She doesn't belong with this group, and she can't stay alone. She's frightened; you know that. By the time we get back—"

"All right, you win." Alison remembered the stricken look on Alison Two's face every time the girl thought of the future. "She *does* need me, and she *can't* go with the rest of you. But if that weren't so—"

"I'd let you fight it out with Holcomb."

The next morning, Aunt Rose stormed at them during

breakfast. "I'd like to know what that new friend of yours thinks he's doing!"

"Holcomb?" said Eric.

"Is that his name? Last evening I found him down in the basement pawing through the laundry like he was some kind of inspector of dirty clothes or something. I told him if he wanted to know anything about our wash to see you!"

Alison and Eric looked at each other. Eric laughed in some bewilderment. "He asked to go out the back way last night. He must have gone down to the basement on the way out. Heaven only knows what he thought he might find in our laundry."

"He was making like Sherlock Holmes," said Alison.

"Who is Sherlock Holmes?" asked Alison Two.

"He's a fictional detective in some stories written long ago. He could look at the mud on a stranger's feet and tell what the man had for breakfast, how old his mother-in-law was, and what dentist his wife patronized. Things like that."

Alison Two laughed. "I don't believe it. How could he?"

"Maybe not quite that good, but pretty close."

"And you think Mr. Holcomb can do things like that?"

Eric said. "I think his appearance is deceiving. The CIA people are some of the toughest cookies on earth, and I've got an idea that Jim Holcomb is right up there with the top ones."

The telegram arrived the next afternoon. It was brief:

"Connie's Hamburgers. NYC. Friday 1 p.m. Have two each. No drinks. No fries. Regards. Jim."

Alison read it first. "What in the world?"

Eric took it from her. "Jim wants Three and me to meet him at this hamburger joint in New York City next Friday at one. He's telling us what to order. That's simple."

Alison looked suddenly anxious. "Eric—do you think this is all right? There's something so unreal about it all. This is *Ivy*. There's a baseball game tonight. Tomorrow's the church supper. It isn't Constantinople or Hamburg or Paris."

"I know. But there's not much else we *can* do. Just keep praying—God will take care of us."

"I know," Alison said. "And I will—you know that."

Friday, Alison and Alison Two drove the boys to the airport. The fields along the road were beginning to show traces of green as the newly planted beans and corn were sprouting. Eric had ridden this road on his bicycle many long years ago. Now he was on his way to meet a master spy on some devious corner in one of the world's roughest cities.

The shuttle air service to Chicago out of Ivy's small airport was called Red Devil Airline. It featured flaming red planes with a figure of a devil with wings flying like Superman along the nose of the plane. He was grinning happily and waving his trident.

Eric had never thought much of the airline's image.

He watched their bags being checked carelessly into

115

the baggage hold. Then he squeezed Alison and put his arm around the shoulders of Alison Two. She was trembling in the warm sunlight.

"Be back before you know it." He waved again as he and his clone mounted the short ramp to the plane, an old DC-7.

In a moment, the door was closed. The stewardess made her little speech about oxygen masks and emergency doors.

The clone, in the window seat, watched the ground drop away as the noisy engines roared a kind of defiance that they still had life in them. The world didn't belong entirely to jets.

They landed in Chicago and changed planes for New York. The clone said scarcely a word, but his eyes scanned everything as if imprinting the sights indelibly in his mind for future reference. In a little more than an hour, they landed at Kennedy.

It was old familiar territory to Eric. He moved them quickly through baggage claims and then sought a phone booth to check for the location of Connie's Hamburgers.

"It's right near Times Square," he said.

"I suppose you know where that is?"

"Yes," said Eric. "It used to be a great place, people tell me. Now it's taken over mostly by druggies and small-time thugs. It's a great place not to be at night."

He led the clone to the taxi line and maneuvered his way skillfully through the mob to a car. He gave the driver the address and settled back. He glanced at his

116

watch. "A little over two hours. Aunt Rose will be serving lunch for the girls."

Noontime crowds still paraded the streets and avenues. "Right here will do," he told the driver. The cab lurched to a stop. Eric gave him fare and a tip.

Eric watched his look-alike standing at the edge of the sidewalk, staring at the crowds like a country boy in the big city for the first time. He smiled a little at the clone's obvious amazement at the congestion and hustle.

"I never knew there were so many people."

"Wait 'til you get where we're going."


The rendezvous was two blocks off Times Square. Eric led the way. It was a neat, white-front place done in Colonial style. There was walk-in service, with a small inside seating area. The two boys got in the long lunch line.

At last they reached the order counter. "Two each," said Eric. "No drinks. No fries."

The counterman never looked up. He hustled the burgers in two packages and snapped, "Five-sixty."

Eric laid down the bills. Change tumbled in the hopper. The counterman snarled to the next customer, "Come on, Mac! We start serving supper in ten minutes. Do you want lunch or not?" Then, with only a slight lowering of his voice and a faint inclination of his head to Eric, he said, "Two doors north. Peter."

The seating was full. They found a small place against the wall and leaned against it. Eric warned the clone to

117

keep his foot against his bags, which were between him and the wall.

Eric chewed the hamburger reluctantly. "Sam, back in Ivy, does better than this."

They finished and sauntered out to the curb in front of the place. Eric looked for the spot two doors north. It was a secondhand bookstore.

He beckoned to his companion and led the way to the door. A bell tinkled somewhere as he pushed the door open. It was like entering a cave. Moments later, a gnome-like creature emerged from the dimness. He gave the boys an owlish stare, pushing his rimless spectacles up high on a forehead that had no perceptible boundary with the nearly hairless scalp. The forehead wrinkled deeply as the little man tried to adjust his eyes.

"Ah, yes," he said finally. "A fine day, is it not?"

"Yeah," said Eric. "It's a great day—a real great day."

"And the ivy is a wonderful plant is it not? So persevering, so tenacious, you might say. Don't you think so?" His eyes went from Eric to the clone and back again, as if he were trying to decide whether he had double vision or not. He kept fingering the pockets of the dirty black vest that he wore unbuttoned.

"Yes, indeed," he said.

"Well—" Eric swallowed. Jim Holcomb had sure left something out of his telegram. What was expected next? "I certainly have to agree with you. The ivy is an excellent plant. One of my favorites. It's the name of my home town, too. Ivy, a great plant, a great town."

The gnome-like man smiled. He seemed satisfied. "I'm so glad you agree," he said. "Just come this way, please."

He led the way into the depths between the dusty shelves that towered nearly to the high ceiling. Two or three customers in the narrow passage looked up in irritation as the three paraded past them. Against the dark back wall of the store, the proprietor fumbled in the depths of a pocket and came up with a ring of keys. He tried two, and then a door opened.

"Come in, please."

Eric didn't know what he expected, but it was nothing. They were in a dark hallway. The man closed the door, locked it carefully and pulled a string to turn on a dim light far above their heads. "This way," he said and led them on.

At the end of the dark tube of the hallway, he fumbled again for keys and at last opened another door. He ushered them in.

The small room reminded Eric of an old-time barber shop that hadn't been cleaned out for months. There was a worn barber's chair in the center of the room. A barber's mirror and cabinets lined the far wall. The mirror was cracked; a piece had fallen out long ago.

The linoleum floor was worn and bulging. A couple of old kitchen chairs with green paint, badly chipped, stood against the wall to the left. Their legs were wired for reinforcement.

"Please be seated over there." The man gestured to the chairs. He seemed utterly perplexed. He took two photographs from the barber's cabinet and approached the boys. "I just don't understand." He shook his head. "I just don't understand which is to be which."

"What is it?" said Eric. "If you'd tell us why we are here—"

"These," the man said. He turned the pictures so that Eric and the clone could see them. "Which of you is to be which?"

With a sudden burst of insight Eric understood. The pictures were of two men, one about thirty and the other a little older. The younger had a small moustache. The older was clean shaven but wore glasses and close-cropped hair. His face was somehow patched with age.

Eric understood that they were to become the men in the pictures. The clone nodded as he grasped the situation, also.

"The older one," he said. "That is I."

The little gnome nodded and went to work.

# 9 • *London*

It took all afternoon, although his movements were swift, industrious, and skilled. He worked on them both at the same time. First, the hair. He combed out Eric's and trimmed it differently. Then he applied a dye that lightened and turned it brown. He clipped the clone's short and sprinkled it with silver.

Then the faces. Eric's moustache, the eyes, the ears, the neck. The clock on the wall, an old-fashioned Regulator with pendulum and hand-wind key, chimed five. It was right, according to Eric's watch.

"We must hurry," the little man said, almost his first words since he started. "But we are almost finished."

In another ten minutes, he backed away with satisfaction and offered a mirror. "Very good, is it not?" he smiled with self satisfaction.

"Very good," said Eric. "Now perhaps you can tell us what this is all about."

He stood back and put up his hands as if in horror.

121

"About? I know nothing. Peter Grutmann knows nothing."

"All right," said Eric. "I guess we're ready to go. He glanced in the big mirror, almost unable to recognize the stranger that was himself.

"You wait. Ten minutes more," said the little man. "I must tell you how to keep up appearances." He laughed. "You understand what I mean?"

He went on to describe how to maintain the disguises. He gave them each a little kit of materials, but assured them little attention need be given for at least six weeks. "Even in the bath," he said, "you are safe."

*Safe from what?* Eric wondered. This elaborate preparation was far more than he had bargained for. In all his previous travels, he had never had to resort to such disguise.

"I presume you are already paid?" he said to Peter Grutmann.

The little man grinned. "Very well. Very well, indeed. You think I could live on selling old books that nobody wants to read anymore?"

Finally, he gave them each an envelope and instructed them to open it and familiarize themselves with the contents. There were airplane tickets to Cairo via London. Eric hadn't known that was their destination. There were passports with pictures of their new images. There were new names. Eric was Joseph Eldredge. The clone was Martin Autusky.

They walked out of the bookstore into the evening

traffic, which was even greater than the noon traffic had been.

The airport hustle, the racket of irritated humanity, and the long waiting lines were put behind them as the 747 left the runway and lifted into the evening lighted by a full moon. Dinner was served and afterwards a movie was turned on.

The clone exclaimed and laughed aloud. "*That* is out there—" He gestured to the window where tall castles of clouds mysteriously lit by the full moon drifted by. "*That* is out there," he said, "and they want to show us a movie!"

Eric shushed him gently. "Not everyone has a window seat. Most of the people can't see outside."

"I guess that's right." The clone relaxed lower in his seat, subdued.

"And besides," said Eric, "most of them wouldn't want to watch cloud castles in the moonlight for six hours, anyway. They'd *rather* see a movie."

But the clone *did* watch the cloud castles. He thought there could be nothing on earth so utterly beautiful as those fantastic shapes that soared in the moonlit night. Their towers reached for the stars, while gold and silver light crept between their mysterious walls and minarets. He held a hand to the side of his face so he wouldn't have to see the silliness on the movie screen.

It was very early morning when the announcement of their impending arrival at London's Heathrow Airport came over the speaker. They felt the plane's descent as it dropped in stages, one, two thousand feet at a time.

Passengers began gathering their paraphernalia and checking their seatbelts according to the instruction of the lighted sign on the bulkhead. Flight attendants walked up and down the aisle checking their charges.

Then the speaker came to life unexpectedly. "Will passenger Mr. Joseph Eldredge please report to the Airport Information Desk on arrival. Mr. Joseph Eldredge, please report—"

The boys looked at each other in silent questioning. What was going on, anyway? Eric understood nothing of how all this was going to help trap Eric Two. He was beginning to resent all the uncertainty surrounding their movements.

The giant plane slid out of the sky and landed smoothly in a light rain and fog. When it had rolled to a final stop, the boys joined the log jam of passengers impatient to be out of the monstrous capsule.

They emerged and streamed more rapidly down the long corridor leading to Baggage Claims and the murky air of London. Eric stopped beside an attendant who seemed watching the crowd as if for smugglers or illegal aliens. "Can you tell me where the information desk is?"

Without taking his eye off the crowd, the man pointed. "End of the corridor. On your right as you leave the baggage carousel."

There was a letter there addressed to Mr. Joseph Eldredge. "May I see some identification, please?" The girl at the counter asked patiently. Eric displayed the passport given him by Grutmann. She examined it, smiled approval, and handed over the envelope. "Have a good visit, Mr. Eldredge."

"Thank you," said Eric.

They moved to a quiet spot away from the streaming passengers. Using the clone as a shield against any accidental glimpse of some bypasser, Eric opened the envelope. It read: "Take room *alone* the 23rd and 24th, 167 Claridge Place. Then proceed to Cairo unless otherwise directed."

Eric looked up. " 'Alone' it says. He wants me to stay here for two days alone. That means you go on to Cairo alone. I'll met you there two days later."

The clone slapped a fist against his palm in disgust and impatience. "And what am I supposed to do while I'm waiting for you? We're wasting time and getting nowhere. This isn't putting us on the trail of Two!"

Eric admitted his bewilderment. "I don't know where it's leading us. I guess I'm supposed to find something critical at this address. What am *I* supposed to do for two days while I wait *here?* We seem to be on a track now and don't know where it's heading, and there seems to be no way to get off."

He tried to conceal the depth of his own frustrations. His friend was depressed enough. "I'm sure Jim will meet us in Cairo," Eric said, "and have some news for us. Let's take it easy until then and see what comes. I know Jim's got a reason for what he's doing."

Eric waited with the clone until the Cairo plane was ready. It was a three-hour wait. They put their bags in lockers and slumped in the waiting-room seats, taking turns at napping and keeping alert for signs of anyone's showing interest in them.

The plane was called at last, and they moved toward the gate. "Just go to the hotel," said Eric. "You've already got the reservation. Don't go anywhere else unless you have some word from Jim Holcomb. Don't talk to anybody. If I'm not going to be there on schedule, I'll let you know." •

The clone grinned. "In other words, you're telling me, 'Don't get lost.' "

Eric touched his arm in a friendly grip. "Something like that. See you in Cairo in a couple of days."

The address given Eric in the letter was six or seven miles from the airport. It was a rundown Victorian house converted to flats. From the cab window, Eric looked at it distastefully and wondered again what he was doing there.

"Is this where you want, Jack?" the cab driver demanded impatiently. "I got other places to go."

"Yes, this is it—I guess." Eric paid him and stepped out into the light fog with his bags. The cab roared away.

At the door, Eric pressed the button. The door opened as if the landlady had been peeking through the curtain of the glass to see who it was. She didn't wait for him to announce himself.

"Are you Mr. Eldredge?" She was a round-faced, middle-aged woman with a motherly beam on her face.

"Yes, I'm Mr. Eldredge," said Eric. "I believe a room was reserved for me here."

"Oh, yes, it was! The room belongs to Mr. Cutler, but he said he'd be gone a few days and you could use it while he was gone. Today and tomorrow, I believe he said. Is that right?"

*And who is Mr. Cutler?* Eric asked himself as he climbed the stairs behind the motherly landlady. "I'm Mrs. Williams," she said. "I wish you were going to stay longer. I always like to get acquainted with my people. I'll bring you some breakfast muffins. You haven't had breakfast yet, have you?"

There was no sign of a Mr. Cutler in the room, Eric found. The closets were empty. The bureau drawers had nothing in them. Whoever Mr. Cutler was, he had taken everything with him. Eric gave up thinking about it and resigned himself to two days of boredom. But, then, he thought, there had to be a purpose in his being here. Somebody for him to meet? Some word of Eric Two to be passed on? He wondered whether Two had already passed through London and had been picked up by Holcomb's men. That didn't make sense, however, or Three would not have been allowed to go on to Cairo.

One thing he was certain of: Jim Holcomb was not stupid. There was a purpose in his being there. He only wished he knew what it was.

He settled down in a chair with a book he had brought and resigned himself to the waiting. Mrs. Williams brought him muffins. In the afternoon, she brought him tea and cakes. "I'd ask you to have supper with us, but I gave up the boarding house business two years ago.

My back, you know. I just couldn't do all that cooking every day."

"I wouldn't expect it," said Eric. "Perhaps you could recommend a place."

"There's a nice little place just around the corner to your right as you step out. They serve American style meals at good prices. You *are* American, aren't you?"

"Yes. If by chance I should have any visitors while I'm out, I would appreciate it if you would take a message. Tell them I'll be only a few minutes."

"Oh! I almost forgot . I was to tell you that you might expect a gentleman between two and four, either today or tomorrow. How could I forget such a thing? It's already past that time for today. Mr. Cutler said it would be quite important."

"I see. Well, thanks, Mrs. Williams. I'll make sure I'm here tomorrow at that time."

He found the restaurant Mrs. Williams recommended. Its American food turned out to be a poor relation to Sam's hamburgers at an exorbitant price. He paid reluctantly and returned to the room.

"You can come down and watch our telly," said Mrs. Williams when he came back. "There are some good American shows on tonight."

"Thanks, but I have a little reading to do, and then I'll be turning in early. A tiring trip over, you know."

"Of course. Goodnight."

He slept late the next morning, took a shower, and went out to find another restaurant. He had better luck with standard English fare instead of imitation American. He returned to the room, gathered what few things he had used, and returned them to his bags—all except the book.

At three o'clock, he heard the bell on the floor below. In a moment Mrs. Williams was calling up the stairwell. "Mr. Eldredge! Mr. Eldredge—a visitor to see you!"

Eric put the book down and waited. The knock came a moment later. He opened to a middle-aged man about his own height. Eric sensed in him some kind of officialdom.

"Your good landlady spares her tenants any surprises with respect to visitors," the man said. He sounded as if he were trying to make light talk, but he did not smile.

"Come in," said Eric. "Have a seat over there."

The visitor stepped inside the doorway but remained standing as Eric closed the door behind him. The man dug into the inner pocket of his suit coat. "I'll only take a moment. It's good of you to give us your time." He pulled out a pair of photographs and opened them up to Eric. "Can you recognize this person?"

The pictures were of the same man. A total stranger. Eric looked blankly at his visitor. "I've never seen him." He shook his head. "Nothing—the pictures mean nothing at all to me."

The man held them a moment longer, as if with persistence he might call forth some recognition from Eric. But Eric shook his head again. "Never have seen him."

The man looked quite disappointed. "I was afraid it would turn out that way. But thanks very much anyway for giving us your time," he said. "You will be properly compensated. Good day, sir."

He turned and left, closing the door carefully behind him. Eric let out a deep breath in frustration and bewilderment. He went to the window and watched the man get in the driver's side of a small Fiat parked a little way down the street from the house. The car drove away quite rapidly.

*So that was the end of the episode. And what was it all about?* he asked himself. *Who made the arrangement for the room? The mysterious Mr. Cutler has to be a member of Jim Holcomb's staff. And who was the stranger with the photographs? Scotland Yard? One of Holcomb's people who thought he had picked up Eric Two?*

He gave it up. But of one thing he was certain: Holcomb had a purpose. There was a purpose in all this that was so deep that merely looking at surface appearances was utterly futile.

*I wonder how Three's doing with his Cairo arrangements,* he thought.

# 10 • Another Assignment

The clone found it a strange experience to be riding without companionship over Europe in the 727 headed for Cairo. There would be one intermediate stop at Tel Aviv.

His territory since infancy had been the ramshackled premises of Swykert's place outside Ivy. Until a few days ago, he had never traveled more than a few hundred yards from that place. He had been aware of the world in books and in pictures. From them, he knew the geography of the whole world by heart. But now he was in it, he thought. All by himself.

He forgot time. He forgot how little of it was left to him. The *now* of flying high above the world with all the tiny villages and cities peeping occasionally through the clouds—this was *now*.

But it changed. The sun lowered in the western sky, and the aircraft sped over the Mediterranean. He remembered seeing it on maps and knew what it was. The captain announced the descent to Cairo Airport. The clone felt a touch of panic. He knew what he should do, but he wasn't sure he could do it.

He plucked his bags off the carousel as they had done at London. Outside, the line of taxi drivers were shouting in what seemed a dozen different languages. He heard a trace of English and rushed for that man. "Hilton," he said. They had reservations for the Nile Hilton. The driver understood and took off like a thunderbolt, weaving like a madman through the honking traffic.

It wasn't a long ride. The driver stopped and opened the door, grinning. "Fast, eh," he said.

The clone nodded in relief and paid the man twice the exorbitant fare he had asked for.

The cab moved away, and the clone stood uncertainly with his bags. The heat pounded against him. Cars moved along the streets in front of the hotel just as cars did in Ivy and New York City. He recognized American makes and Japanese, which he had seen before. Many he had never seen. Pedestrians moved over the crosswalks, dressed in a variety of clothing. Some in business suits, which looked familiar; others in foreign dress he had never seen. A number, he guessed, were in police or military uniform.

The hotel rose a dozen stories beside him, its white, concrete balconies stacked against a blue sky. Clusters of trees and shrubs huddled between it and the street traffic. Beyond, a stately stone lion guarded the approach to a bridge over the Nile.

He turned and strode confidently into the lobby of the hotel. He spotted the registration desk and presented the reservation form that had been included in the packet given him in New York. "Mr. Autusky," he said. "Mr. Eldredge and I are together. He will be along a little later."

The clerk checked his cards and nodded. "Yes, we've already been informed of Mr. Eldredge's delay. We will hold the adjoining room for his arrival."

*Informed already*, the clone thought. *Holcomb is thorough. His people certainly have taken care of all the details.*

The clerk placed a registration form in front of him. He filled out his name as Martin Autusky. On the line, *Company:* he wrote, Carson Electronics, Cincinnati, Ohio. That instruction was in the packet, too. He went up to the room, unaware that carrying his bags was a service he was expected to pay for, but he caught on with the porter's persistence.

He shut the door and stood by the window, viewing the desert city below. It was an immense place. Nearly six million inhabitants, Eric had told him during the flight. And so *old*. To the west, he saw through the light haze the three pyramids of Giza.

He had read about the pyramids. Built by men who did not want to die. But they had died anyway. Five thousand years ago. And the great piles of stone were monuments to nothing but their folly.

He inspected the room carefully, taking note of all things unfamiliar to him. The furniture was not unusual.

He inspected the bathroom. It was similar to the one at Eric's house—in function, at least. There was the telephone. He had not actually used one, but he had seen it done often enough that he was sure he knew how. He understood the purpose of the directory.

He was most uncertain of the eating arrangements. He was aware of the variety of restaurants, but he had seen the inside of none except the hamburger place in New York and the one in Ivy, where he and Eric and the girls had eaten on the way to the airport. He was aware there were many kinds of food he did not know the names of. He wondered where he could get a hamburger.

Toward evening, he took the elevator and wandered slowly through the lobby of the hotel, listening to its burble of sounds, voices speaking in unknown tongues, smelling the exotic scent of flowers and tobaccos, all strange to his senses, watching the people of nationalities and dress he had never imagined.

He found a restaurant. He looked in upon its formal and complex dining and was frightened away. Then he found the coffee shop. It had a row of stools and a counter. It looked like a hamburger shop. He cautiously entered, looking for a list of items served. He found a menu and sat on a stool. He felt an almost delirious excitement when he saw the familiar word, hamburger. He ordered two and a soft drink.

He sat on the end farthest from the door. There were only two or three others at the counter. As the waitress brought his order, he became conscious of another customer who slid onto the stool two seats away. The man was broad and heavy. He wiped his thick, moist neck with a white handkerchief as he scanned the menu. He turned and offered a friendly smile when he saw the clone observing him.

"Hot country," he said. "Hard to get used to at first. Just get in today?"

The clone hesitated. He remembered Eric's caution not to speak to anyone. That was nonsense! He nodded to the stranger.

"American, I'll bet," the man said.

He nodded again. He needed to try out his ability to cope with strangers, "You, too?" he said.

The man laughed. "No. I don't look like an American, I'm afraid. Ankara—Turkey. But I speak good English, don't I?"

"Very good. I'm not familiar with people of other countries. It's hard for me to tell."

"Well, don't let that bother you. In this part of the world a person is liable to be from anywhere—or nowhere."

The waitress poised for the stranger's order.

"I like the looks of those American-type hamburgers. I think I'll have a couple of them myself." She wrote on her pad and disappeared.

"I was in New York once," said the man. "Flew all the way out to San Francisco, too. Great country, America. People don't know how good they've got it there. You vacationing—or on business?"

The clone took a large bite of his hamburger and a

135

drink to soak it down. He remembered the company name of his identification. "Electronics business," he said. "Mathematician."

"Oh—that's a good field," the man said. "I'll bet you can sell buckets of goods to these people around here—provided you can beat out the Japanese. They're tough competitors the whole world around."

The clone finished his second hamburger and slid off the stool. He remembered and went back to leave the waitress a tip.

"Are you staying long?" he asked the man.

"I'll be here for quite a while, I suppose. Maybe I'll see you again. I'd like to talk to you about the electronics business. That's something we need badly in Turkey. We import everything—that's not good."

"I'll be here a few days."

He paid the cashier. In the mirror behind her, he saw the stranger was still watching him.

In his room, the clone tried to find some suitable music on the radio or TV. It was hopeless. He drew out of his bag a couple of mathematical texts he had brought along. This was his primary love, the thing that excited him most. He took out a thick writing pad and a ball point pen. He opened the texts and scanned some references. Then he began writing on the pad. He kept at it, writing faster and faster until darkness covered the city and only the lights of the high-rise apartments shone through his window. He drew the curtains and turned on the lights and went on with his writing.

He surprised himself by how well he slept that night.

He woke up refreshed and feeling like exploring the strange city. He wouldn't go far, of course. Just a walk around a nearby block or two. He wondered if he might run into the man from Ankara.

After showering and dressing, he went down to the coffee shop. He remembered the bacon and eggs Mrs. Jenkins served at the Thornes' and tried ordering a breakfast like theirs. It turned out very well.

As he paid for his meal, he remembered Eric would be in that day, but it would probably be late. He had almost the whole day ahead of him. He'd have a lot of time for his writing.

It was a good time to walk around. The air was hot, but the sun was not high. He stepped out of the hotel and sauntered down the street. Standing in the shade of a plane tree a couple of hundred feet away was his acquaintance of the night before. In the sunlight, he looked older. Maybe fifty. The clone felt a gladness at meeting someone he knew.

The man was smoking a long cigar. The drifting smoke smelled strangely different than any the clone had encountered before. Looking up, the man removed the cigar and waved in friendly recognition.

"Good morning! I see you Americans are anxious to take advantage of the early coolness, such as it is."

"You were right," the clone said. "This is a hot country."

"I should have introduced myself last night. I am Anton Petrark, importer."

"I'm Martin Autusky."

"That's not a very American sounding name," said Petrark. He laughed gently, and his belly rippled in waves.

"My ancestors must have come from—somewhere. I've never looked it up."

"Shall we walk?"

The clone fell in step beside his new acquaintance. He hadn't realized before how big the man's girth really was. Petrark was a head shorter than he, but his waist line must have been more than twice the size of his own. He walked, however, with a kind of side-to-side sway of his hips that was graceful in its way and enabled him to navigate his huge bulk at a good pace. The clone didn't have to slow down at all.

"Tell me," Anton Petrark said, "do you think it would be possible to establish a real electronics industry in a country like mine?"

The clone fumbled for words. "I don't see why not. I don't know much about Turkey, but every country today has use for radios, TVs, computers. There's no country with a decent, intelligent labor supply that can't build its own goods more cheaply than importing them."

"That's exactly what I've been saying to our ministers of trade and finance, but they keep telling me we don't know how to do such things. We have to depend on others."

"Education, then," the clone suggested.

They discussed it for several blocks and finally wound back to the hotel.

Anton Petrark stopped in the shade again. "You

spoke of education," he said gravely. "We are much in need of educational information. Perhaps you have something you would be willing to let us have—for a good consideration, of course."

"I don't know what you mean."

"Oh, come now! I do business with people like you every week. If you really want to know, that is my *main* business. You know, information that isn't really permitted under trade and security agreements, but which young fellows—engineers like you—carry around in their heads. Some of them make a great deal of money like that. And tax-free, of course."

"I'm not an engineer. Mathematics—"

"Very often just the thing we need! Give it a little thought and see if there isn't something you believe would be of use to us."

Eric's flight from London landed at Cairo Airport late in the afternoon. He hadn't told his friend the time of his arrival. He took a cab to the hotel and slammed into his room without warning. He dumped his luggage on the floor and opened the connecting door to see whether his companion was in his room.

The clone had been startled by the noise from Eric's room and was sitting upright, the pad of paper on his knee, when Eric burst into the room and flopped on the bed in exhaustion.

"I wasn't expecting you," he said.

"I wanted to get off that wild goose chase as fast as I could," Eric said. "I just don't know. I'd sure like to

have a chat with Mr. Jim Holcomb right about now.''
He sat up. "Anyway, I got the earliest flight I could out
of London. I was lucky. But then—maybe not.'' He
took off his coat. "I had forgotten how hot it was here,
and that the plague of flies never really left Egypt after
Moses' time. How has it been with you?''

The clone shrugged. "I've been quite comfortable
here in the room. I only went out to eat. But you're
going to have to show me how to order food at a restaurant. There must be something besides hamburgers and
eggs and bacon.''

Eric laughed. "You should try the British version!''
He looked about the room and crossed to close the
drapes against the blazing red disc of the sun beyond
the pyramids. He glanced at the pad of mathematical
symbols. "What's that? You look like you're cramming
for a final exam or something.''

The clone lifted one of the math books. "I brought
along a few things to keep me occupied in case there
was any idle time, and there *has* been plenty of that!
What did you do in London?''

Eric told him. "It was all set up, just like in a spy
story. Meeting with a secret agent and all that sort of
stuff. I never did figure it out, but what I think is that
somebody got over-anxious to make some points with
headquarters. So when he got Jim's message about
being on the watch for Two, this bird thought he had
him spotted. The picture I was shown was so far off it
was funny. It looked like something they must have dug
out of their police files a hundred years old. And when I

142

told the old boy I'd never seen the person in the picture, I thought he was going to cry."

"I still think Jim Holcomb is not a very bright man."

"I don't agree." Eric paused. "I was mad about what seemed like a runaround in London—I still am, I guess. But there was more to it than that. Something was accomplished. I don't know what it was. Holcomb has got something going. I think we're going to be quite surprised when we find out what."

"How about dinner?"

"I'm with you. I passed up that stuff they had on the airplane. I'll show you how to order a steak—if you can still get one here."

Eric remembered that on his last visit, the steaks were good. He didn't know where they came from, but the price indicated they were probably flown in. He ordered for them both. Then, while they waited, he explained the intricacies of the menu.

When their orders came, the clone shook his head in sad reminiscence. "We never ate like this at Swykert's. He brought home a steak—just once, a long time ago. We couldn't eat it. He said it was made of shoe leather. We didn't understand what he meant."

Eric laughed. "Just a joke. There are steaks—and there are steaks."

The clone thought he saw Petrark once, but decided it couldn't be he. He hoped the man wouldn't come around while he was with Eric.

"I hope this is on the expense account," said Eric.

Holcomb had given them a few hundred dollars for pocket money. Eric reached for the bill. Under it was a smaller piece of paper.

Eric glanced at his friend and then back at the paper. He turned it over carefully, hiding it with the bill. On it was written a phone number and the notation: Pay phone #8.

"I guess I have to make a phone call," Eric said. "Stand by me." Holcomb was on the other end. "Listen," he said. "Don't talk."

"London—"

"Don't talk!" Holcomb's voice was sharp.

Eric remained silent.

"Check at the registration desk," said Holcomb. "Priority mail." Holcomb hung up. Eric replaced the phone.

The clone had been waiting, barring the entrance to the booth. "Anything?" he asked.

Eric nodded silently and led the way to the lobby and to the registration desk.

"Joseph Eldredge," Eric said. "Priority mail."

The expressionless clerk looked at him, then reached beneath the desk and brought up a pad of forms. "Sign here, please."

The clerk watched. He glanced at the signature. "One moment, sir." He disappeared through a doorway into a back room.

The clerk returned in a moment with a brown envelope marked "Joseph Eldredge."

"Have a good evening, sir," the clerk said.

"Eric stuffed the envelope in his pocket, and the two boys returned to their rooms. Eric locked the door behind them and tore open the envelope. In bold letters at the top were the words: No talk. Room may be bugged.

Eric showed it to the clone, who looked puzzled and started to open his mouth. Eric clapped a hand over his face and put a finger to his own lips. The other boy nodded.

They went on reading. "Eric will prepare for three days' absence. Go to Hassam's House of Seven Camels on El Caife Street. Ask for Hassam. Three remain at hotel."

At the last line, the clone started to explode. Eric clapped a hand over his mouth again and the clone subsided. Eric inclined his head toward the doorway.

They returned to the lobby and went outside. The hotel grounds and nearby streets were well lighted. Eric steered away from other pedestrians.

"I'm not going to sit alone in that hotel room another three days!" the clone burst out. "I might as well go back home. I could at least be working on my research there. So little time for me—and so much waste!"

Eric spread his hands helplessly. "I'm sorry," he said. "I can't do anything about it now. We've just got to trust Holcomb. When we get in touch with him again, we'll tell him how you feel. Maybe he's got a part for you to play in this yet."

The clone subsided. "I'm sorry, Eric. I didn't mean to blow up at you. I know it's not your fault. You're not in control of things. But I keep thinking: if just you and I

145

looked at this problem and tackled it our own way, we could do it."

"What would we do? Do you know where to find Two?"

"Yes—I'm sure I do. He's not here, not in Egypt. He's where I said first. He would go to Saudi Arabia. There, in Riyadh, he's probably right now in contact with Soviet agents, telling them the Americans are preparing to station themselves in the country to take over the oil fields. And he's probably telling the Saudis that the Russians are planning an invasion very soon, so that the Saudis will try to get the Americans to keep the Russians out. That's the kind of thing he is telling them."

"What about his weapon, the EMR projector?"

"When he's got them all stirred up, he will give it to one or the other. The Russians, I am sure. They're the ones that would use it most recklessly. When that happens, the Americans will be forced to use their bombs. That's the way it will all end—the way Two wants it."

"As I said before, they're not dummies. Neither side. They know that game. They wouldn't get sucked in that easily."

"You'll see. You don't know Two," said the clone furiously. "He *knows* how to make them believe. He can do it!"

"All right. So what do you think we should do?"

"Leave! Leave now. Forget Holcomb and his games and go to Riyadh ourselves. We can find Two there. I know. I know how he thinks."

146

Eric sighed wearily. *Maybe Three is right,* he thought. *Who can know?* But he didn't believe Jim Holcomb was as incompetent as his friend thought. A man didn't reach his position in the world of intrigue and treachery on the basis of stupidity. He was clever, Eric thought; he had to be clever. His moves had meaning and purpose.

"Let's play this one more hand," said Eric. "Let's find out what Holcomb is up to this one time. When we get to him, we'll pin him down and tell him what you've just said. Then we'll take it from there. O.K.?"

"All right." The clone seemed deflated. "We'll do that. He looked up at the sky, the distant stars clear in the desert sky. "You have so much time—I have so little."

# 11 • Mr. Sessim

The location Eric was given was in the bazaar section of the city, where hundreds of shouting, pleading vendors hawked their wares for the tourists. He took a cab as far as he could, then went on foot. This was the worst of Cairo, the worst of Egypt. The smells, the flies, the dirt, and the crashing jostling of animals and people were almost terrifying.

In some areas, the vendors' stalls were mere flimsy tents with scarves, brassware, jewelry, and phony antiques hung from the supporting ropes and strewn about the entrance. The cries of the vendors were an endless, monotonous singsong inviting the unwary tourist to view their incredible treasures.

Eric took the route the cab driver had prescribed. He found no House of Seven Camels. He asked half a dozen vendors and got blank stares and a sudden inability to speak English. Finally, one tourist overheard him and laughed. He was an American with a jaunty English cap tilted on his head. "You won't get these fellows to tell you where anybody else's stall is. After all, they want you to buy their junk, not his."

"I've got to find—"

"It's two streets down and then to your left. Go straight ahead there until you come to an area of adobe buildings. There, you go right a half block and you'll be in front of Hassam's place. But you don't want to do business with him. I know—I just got taken for a real ride. Stay away from Hassam and his Seven Camels," the stranger advised. With a laugh, he waved and walked off.

Eric followed the directions and found himself in front of the adobe structure. It was open on the ground level, with a tent awning extending out into the street. A lone camel squatted on the ground beside the awning. The smell was almost something that could be seen, Eric thought.

Eric approached Hassam's. He picked up a brass piece and wondered whether Alison would like that. Then he remembered her distaste for tourist souvenirs. He put it down.

"Very fine piece, yes?" A grinning man with long, protruding front teeth approached. "Very good price for the American," he said.

"I am looking for Hassam," said Eric.

"Ah, but he is not about yet. So early in the morning."

"Please tell him Joseph Eldredge has arrived."

The man bowed low and touched the rim of his dusty

turban. "Of course, sir. He will be informed at once, sir."

The man disappeared. Eric waited in the hot shade of the tent flap. Two women watched from the rear of the building. The camel dozed in the heat. A pair of yowling dogs ran between the stream of tourists in the street.

"He will see you at once, Mr. Eldredge." The shopkeeper was by his side abruptly. "If you will follow me, please—"

They went through a curtain at the back of the shop, stepping between the two women, who refused to move. The guide led the way up a rickety stairway leading to the upper floor of the adobe building. At a dusty landing, he opened a door. "Hassam will see you, Mr. Eldredge." He bowed and left.

Eric stepped cautiously toward the door. Seated inside, cross-legged on a pile of pillows of several velvet colors, an old man stared back at him. The man's face was dark as a pecan and wrinkled deeply. In contrast, his beard seemed snow white. The turban on his head, as well as the robe on his shoulders, was white, as if untouched by the yellow desert sands.

"Come in, Mr. Eldredge," he said in a deep, pleasant voice. His English had only a trace of Arabic accent.

Eric entered. The door slammed shut behind him in the warm desert breeze that burst suddenly through the open window. The old man looked at him a moment, then moved off the sofa. "We must hurry," he said. "There is much to do."

Eric looked around, a sense of apprehension growing

150

within him. *What* was there to do? Then a vague sense of familiarity struck him. He glanced at the cabinet against the wall with its mirror, and the tall stool in front of it. He noticed the scissors and combs and the little boxes of objects.

He was going to be made up again—with still another face!

"This," said the old man. He held up a picture and propped it on the shelf in front of the mirror.

Eric choked down an exclamation. It was a copy of the same picture the agent—or policeman—had shown him in London.

"Please, sit here," Hassam said. "Remove your coat, if you please."

Eric submitted to the work of the aged Egyptian with a complete lack of understanding. He forced himself to believe that this was by Jim Holcomb's orders and that the CIA man knew what he was doing. He knew it was useless to ask the Egyptian questions.

When he was through, Hassam offered Eric a mirror. Eric looked at himself front and back in the double reflection from the cabinet mirror. He had a dark, bushy moustache now. He didn't like that nearly as well as the previous neat and trim one. His hair had some-how been made bushier and pushed lower over his forehead. It was quite black. Something had been done to his jowls. He looked like a pudgy, middle-aged man, he thought.

"You are Mr. Sessim," said the Egyptian. "Listen to me carefully and remember. You are Turkish. You buy

151

and sell wheat. You are on a tour of the countryside inspecting the crops. You will drive about for two days—I will show you where on a map. I will provide you a car.

"On the third day you will go to the pyramid of Maddrah. You are Sessim, the wheat dealer, on his way home. You stop like a tourist and take pictures. Precisely at one o'clock, you will do this. And you will walk around, and you will take some more pictures.

"Between one and one-thirty, a man will come. A cab driver looking for fares back to the city. You will say to him, 'My good man, you are just in time.' You will wave a five-dollar American bill at him and you will say, 'Allow me to take a picture of you by the monument of your ancestors.' "

Eric interrupted. "Is this for real? Do I really have film in the camera and really take these pictures?"

"It is exact," said Hassam. "You do exactly that. I have a camera. I have film. You must have plenty of film. This man will take the bill and then he will sit on the rock by the pyramid and you will take two pictures. When he is gone, you will sit down where he sat to change the roll of film in your camera. And you will see a package, an envelope, where you are sitting, where he sat. You will be careful not to be observed as you slip this into your coat and proceed on your way."

"Where?" said Eric. "What do I do with this envelope? And what has all this got to do with locating—"

The Egyptian raised his eyebrows majestically as if he were a schoolmaster and Eric had just flunked his

152

finals. "You and I," he said, "we are warriors, are we not? We have questions, but we do not ask for answers. We fight on, and in the end, the battle is won—or perhaps it is lost. But we do our parts. Yes?"

"Yes," Eric said humbly, "but what do I do with—"

"I will explain."

Hassam provided different clothes. Not new ones. Far from it. There was a dark suit and a rumpled shirt. They were dirty, and they smelled. Eric would have some strong words with Jim Holcomb if they ever met again.

Hassam took him down the rickety stairs and through a back door to the rear of the building. In the hot sun, with its windows closed, was an ancient 1939 Chevrolet. The tires were spattered with mud and caked sand, but Eric noted they were almost brand new.

"An excellent vehicle," said Hassam, patting it lovingly. "I have driven it myself for the past thirty-five years. It gives no trouble."

Eric prayed that it wouldn't. He had examined the map Hassam had prepared and had a vague idea of the territory he was supposed to cover in his disguise as a wheat merchant. If the ancient car broke down anywhere along that route, he would be done for.

He had to wear a black hat, Hassam had said. It was part of the scene. Mr. Sessim was never without his black hat. Eric kept it on as he steered the car along a sandy road away from the bazaar. He listened carefully to the engine. It sounded good. In the body and the steering, there were no squeaks or rattles. The upholstery was perfect. *Hassam must have kept it under glass and lubricated it weekly since it came off the assembly line,* Eric thought.

He wondered whether there actually was a Mr. Sessim somewhere, who had been detained by Holcomb's people, or if the character of the Turkish wheat merchant was wholly fictitious. He should have asked Hassam.

He drove for several hours, deep into the farming areas upriver from Cairo. Small villages, mostly of adobe huts, were scattered along the way. He sought out the wheat fields and drove slowly along the sandy, rutted roads between them as he had been instructed to do. *This is insane,* he thought. *There is no one within miles to know or care where I am or what I'm doing.* He wiped the sweat from his brow and laid the hot, black hat on the seat.

Then he remembered Hassam's instructions and put it back on again. "Stupid hat," he muttered.

The Egyptian had given him some sheets of information he was supposed to read and memorize as he drove. They had to do with varieties of wheat, the conditions of the plants, and the prices in Cairo, Ankara, and Chicago. He digested the instructions as Hassam had directed.

Near nightfall, he approached a small village identified on his map as Nur, which was to be his first night's stopping place. He closed his eyes momentarily and held his breath as he approached. The goats and the dogs and the sheep and the donkeys had been taken into their owners' houses for the night, but their aroma remained like a cloud over the cluster of huts.

The single inn was the largest building there. Square adobe buildings spread out from there in all directions for about a quarter of a mile. A score of children, some naked, some in rags, followed his car shouting excitedly as their mothers screamed after them from the open doors of the huts.

He entered the stifling atmosphere of the inn. The proprietor was a toothless old man who wore a dirty fez and seemed to speak no English. He got the idea Eric wanted a room and held up his fingers for the price. Eric paid without the usual haggling and went upstairs.

The door was half open, and it wouldn't shut any farther. Eric propped a chair against the knob to hold it as closed as it would go. He threw off the black coat and the steaming hat and flopped on the dust-covered bed—and as abruptly got up again as roaches scattered in all directions.

He slept in the wobbly chair—for such sleep as he got, which was not much. In the morning, the toothless proprietor invited him to breakfast with his family. The menu was goat's meat and goat's milk and a brick-like loaf. The proprietor managed this last with great skill in spite of his lack of teeth. A young girl of about thirteen, who looked as if her eyes could see beyond the horizon of her poverty, spoke some French, and in that language Eric explained his wheat business and his purpose in the area. It seemed the family was already familiar with Mr. Sessim, so Hassam's transformation of Eric into the Turkish merchant must have been accurate. No one looked at him suspiciously. Eric's question about the reality of Mr. Sessim was answered; he wondered what had happened to the real Sessim.

He drove through the fields all that day. Much of the wheat had already been harvested. It all should have been; it was very ripe. He stopped one more night at another village and another inn exactly like the first. He was so exhausted, he wondered for a moment whether he might have stumbled into the same place a second time. But this innkeeper had two long teeth in front, one on the top and one on the bottom. They didn't meet. The smell was the same, and the roaches were as numerous.

The third day he headed for Maddrah, a small pyramid that attracted only a few of the tourists most knowledgeable about Egyptian antiquities. He gauged the distance and allowed himself to arrive a little before one o'clock. The pyramid stood in utter bleakness in a desert that seemed endless on all sides. A single brown road led from whatever civilization was over the horizon. To Eric, it seemed he had traveled from another world to reach this place.

The pyramid of Maddrah had reposed here for nearly 4000 years. It was built of adobe, and it seldom saw rain to leach it away. There was a series of six-feet-high platforms that rose, one on top of another, to a height of over a hundred feet. It was one of the oldest pyramids in Egypt.

A small group of a half dozen tourists clustered at a far corner of the structure, near a small orange bus. Eric avoided them and parked as far away as he could. He walked a few feet through the sand and got out the camera that Hassam had given him. It was a beat-up Nikon F-1.

He began shooting pictures of the pyramid, taking his time between each one. He glanced at his watch. One-fifteen. The unknown courier would have to hurry. Sweat dripped down Eric's face from the edge of the miserable black hat. A drop fell on the camera lens. *Let it stay,* he thought. Then he reconsidered and pulled out the tail of the reeking shirt he wore and wiped the glass.

As he did so, he saw from the corner of his eye a small, distant cloud of dust. He shot a few more frames, carefully watching the dust funnel rising to the sky. Then he was sure. An ancient, wheezing cab became visible. He watched it while he resumed shooting.

It clattered up not far from him and emitted a fountain of steam as the driver shut off the engine.

Impatiently, Eric crunched through the sand toward the man. He'd be more than glad when this was over. He almost forgot to take the five-dollar bill from his pocket.

Remembering, he waved it to the driver. "My good man," he said, "you are just in time. Allow me to take a picture of you by the monument of your ancestors."

The man grinned broadly as he saw the bill. Eric held it out. The man took off his hat and bobbed his head in enthusiastic assent. He moved toward the edge of the stepped pyramid and looked questioningly at Eric, as if for directions.

Eric could see no evidence of a package in the man's possession. Maybe this was the wrong man. Eric didn't have another bill. The man tucked the one Eric had given him somewhere in the depths of the voluminous folds of his clothing. Then he stood still—grinning as if he knew something Eric didn't.

Eric pressed the button.

Then he indicated to the man to sit on a large chunk of adobe that had tumbled from somewhere high up on the pyramid. The man hastily obliged. His teeth showed in a wide yellow display as Eric raised the camera once more.

As abruptly as he had complied, the man's face changed to a look of utter horror. He stood up, pointing a finger at Eric, hooting wildly.

Eric lowered the camera and shouted, "What's the matter?" He noted that *now* there was something on the adobe chunk where the man had sat. A package. An envelope. Whatever—

The man whirled back to the package and apparently pressed his fist against it. Then he ran like the wind toward his ancient car. Eric watched in astonishment, absently noting how easily the clattering engine started. The car roared with an amazing sound and spun sand. Eric hid his face and ducked behind his own car to avoid it. The cab raced away.

At that moment, a faint hissing sound came from the adobe chunk where the package still lay. Eric glimpsed a tiny flame. And then a ball of fire swelled and burst with a roar. Eric flattened to the sand behind the protection of his Chevy. Flaming air thundered over him.

He raised his head in bewilderment. The flame was gone. On the adobe chunk, a blackness marked the spot where the package had been.

An attempt to kill him? Eric wondered. No, that didn't seem to be it. Everything had been all right until the very last moment. Something had spooked the cab driver. He pressed the self-destruct trigger on the package, which was set for that purpose.

But why?

Some signal that Eric had failed to give had alerted the man to the fact that Eric was not the expected courier. But Eric was certain he had done everything Hassam had instructed him to do. Something had gone wrong; he didn't know what.

The small cluster of tourists at the other end of the pyramid had heard the explosion and were coming toward him. He wanted nothing to do with them. He hurried to the blackened adobe and shot a couple of frames. Just for the record. Then he saw a few bits of charred paper, not entirely consumed in their centers. He scooped them up and shoved them into his coat pocket.

He climbed in the Chevy and started the engine as a couple of Americans jogged up.

"Hey, buddy!" they called. "What's going on here?"

He raced down the sandy road leaving them waving their arms in the air.

The car would do a surprising sixty-five on the fairly smooth desert road that paralleled the Nile, but when the pyramid was a few miles behind him, he slowed down. The car did tend to vibrate at that speed.

*Where to, now?* he considered. He had a final rendezvous assigned him, but that seemed purposeless now that he did not have the package to deliver. Jim Holcomb would undoubtedly be upset no end if he didn't make the contact, but he decided to let that happen. Holcomb could call, and he'd be glad to tell him the whole thing had misfired and—what was it all about, anyway? His faith in the CIA operative was being stretched almost as thin as it would go. He just prayed that things would work out.

He headed straight toward Cairo.

It was after dark when he reached the hotel parking lot. He remembered then that all his keys, his identification, all the contents of his pockets of his other clothes had been left with Hassam. He probably was to have picked them up at the last station. He put his arms on the steering wheel and rested his head. His room key could go, but he had to have his passport. There was no way tonight; he was just too tired.

He took the stairway to his floor to avoid riding the elevator in his stinking clothes. There was no one in the hall as he walked quickly down to Three's room. He knocked gently on the door.

"Hey, it's me, Joseph Eldredge," he said, remembering Holcomb's warning. "I lost my keys. Let me in."

After a moment he heard a step inside, then the rattle

of the lock. The clone opened the door cautiously, then tried to slam it shut. But Eric had thrust his body into the crack.

"Hey, it's me," he whispered tensely. "They gave me a new face. It's all right—"

The wary clone relaxed his pressure on the door a trifle. He stared at Eric. "How am I supposed to know that? Who's the larceny detective in Ivy?"

"Ed Mitchell. Now let me in! And keep it down; remember?"

The clone also remembered Holcomb's warning about a bug and released the door. "Look, even Alison or Ed Mitchell wouldn't know you," he said softly. "How do you expect me to? That's a *stupid* moustache. Where have you been?" He wrinkled his nose. "Where *have* you been?"

"Herding goats. I'll get a bath and tell you all about it."

While he was shedding the smelly clothes in his own room, he heard the phone ring in the adjacent room. He stopped, motionless, and listened. The clone said, "Sorry, wrong number."

Eric resumed shedding the clothes. He wondered where he could burn them. It would probably be all right to put them in the hotel trash. He took a quick shower and dried off. While he was searching for fresh clothing of his own, the clone wandered in. "I'd like to go down to the coffee shop for something cool to drink. Any objections?"

"Go ahead."

"Can I bring you something?"

"No. I'm going down for dinner. Did you eat?"

His companion nodded. "I didn't know when you would be here."

"Sure. Why don't you have your drink and wait for me? I'll be down in a few minutes. We can sit to-gether."

After the clone had gone, Eric lay on the bed and closed his eyes for a minute. He couldn't forget the episode at the pyramid. It was too fantastic to believe.

What had it amounted to, anyway? What had been in the package the courier destroyed? What had spooked him into doing that?

Eric sat up. He thought of the bits of paper he had salvaged. They might give a hint of what it was all about. Holcomb would probably like to see those bits—or whoever he should have delivered the package to.

He slipped his hand carefully in the pocket of the smelly black coat. It was dumb to stuff the fragments in like that. They were even more broken and crumbled than when he picked them up. He should have had an envelope.

He drew out what was left of the fragments and laid them carefully on the table beside his bed. None of them was much bigger than a postage stamp. The only large one was maybe two by three inches of unburned paper. He could see it was yellow originally. He leaned down and squinted. There was writing of some kind on the paper. Some foreign language. It wasn't anything familiar to him, not French, not German, not English, certainly. Maybe Farsi. It looked just a little like Arabian characters.

Then he laughed a little at himself. It wasn't any language at all. Not *that* kind, anyway. They were mathematical symbols.

He stopped laughing suddenly and sat very still. His hands were trembling. It took him a little while to get them to stop shaking. It was hard to breathe, too.

He finally arose and carried the piece of paper carefully into the next room. The clone's note pad and open math text were still on the table. Some of his mathematical scrawls were on the top sheet.

Eric held the burned fragment of paper against the note pad. He started trembling all over again. The paper was the same. Yellow notepad with blue lines. The characters were in the same handwriting. The package that had been destroyed consisted of his companion's mathematical equations.

# 12 • Deadly Discovery

Eric found the clone seated at one of the small tables in the coffee shop. "Let's go into the restaurant," he said. "I'm ready for a big feed after three days on goat meat and hard tack."

"What took you so long?"

"Boy, you'll never know how good a bath and bed feel after the goats and the donkeys. You can't get enough of it." He felt he was babbling. He forced himself to stop it. He smiled. "You'll never know, that is, until Holcomb assigns you the next tour of duty among the goats."

They chose a seat in a far corner of the restaurant so they could talk privately.

"Seriously, Eric," said the clone, "why don't we get a plane out of here for Riyadh in the morning and let Holcomb do his own figuring as to what happened to us?"

"I'm not so sure that would work," said Eric. "I've

164

got a feeling that if we tried it, we'd find a net dropping over our heads right at the airport gate.''

"You think he's going to keep a leash on us now?''

"I think he's going to do just that. I fouled up the assignment at the pyramid for him, and I think he's going to be one very unhappy agent.''

"But he's not even on the trail of Two. He hasn't the slightest idea where he is!''

"Maybe he knows more than we think.''

The waitress brought dinner for Eric. The clone waited to join him in dessert.

"Tell me about it,'' he said. "What happened out there?''

Eric glanced around. The nearby tables were unoccupied. In a low voice, he related the happenings of the past three days. He didn't mention collecting the scraps, however.

The clone shook his head. "Doesn't make much sense, does it? What was that business at the pyramid, anyway? And why did he involve you in it? That couldn't possibly have anything to do with us and Two.''

Eric had finished his steak. They were on dessert now. "I'm going to call this number we were given the other day and see whether I can raise Holcomb. We might as well know the worst.''

When they had finished, Eric went to the same phone he had used before. He tried the number and hung up before it was answered.

"Busy,'' he said. He leaned against the edge of the

booth. "I'll try a few more times and see whether I can get through."

His companion shuffled his feet impatiently. "I'll go on up to the room and do some reading. O.K.?"

"Sure. I'll be along soon."

He watched the clone leave and then checked his watch. Eleven o'clock—three in Ivy. He dialed the long distance operator. "I want to reach this number in the United States," he said. "I don't know the prefixes. How long will it take?"

"You are very fortunate, sir. There is usally a minimum wait of two hours, but I can dial for you right now if you will give me the number."

He gave it to her and deposited a pile of change which he had obtained from the cashier. He heard the operator dialing, the clicks of a horde of relays, the final buzz of ringing.

A gruff voice came on. "Police. Larceny Division. Quigley speaking."

Eric said, "I want to speak to Lt. Mitchell."

"Sorry. The lieutenant's tied up right now. I'll have him call you back."

"Listen. This is Eric Thorne. I'm calling from Cairo, Egypt, and it's extremely urgent that I speak to Mr. Mitchell right now. When he hears what I've got to say, he won't be angry with you no matter what you have to interrupt."

"Well—"

"Now!" demanded Eric. "This is costing me bucks."

In a moment the lieutenant came on. "Eric! Is that really you? What's up?"

"Lieutenant, this is important. It's about that fellow that robbed Mr. Barrett. You've never found him, have you?"

"No, we sure haven't. He got clean away. But you aren't calling all the way from Egypt about *him*, are you?"

"It's got something to do with him. I want you to do something for me, Mr. Mitchell. Don't think I'm crazy, but please just do it and let me know the results."

"You sound mysterious. What is this big thing you want done?"

"You know the planing mill down by the creek?"

"Sure."

"On the north side there's a place where a little bluff of white clay sticks out and makes the river go around it. It's the only place around where that white clay is found."

Ed Mitchell chuckled a little. "I know the place you're talking about. Used to be real good fishing in that hole before so many people began using it for a dump."

"O.K. I want you to drag the creek around there and for a couple of hundred yards downstream if you have to."

The lieutenant grunted in disbelief. "Drag the creek? What in the world would we be dragging the creek for?"

"A body," said Eric. "A body, probably with a couple of rocks tied to it."

167

When Ed Mitchell got to the office the next morning, he still had the problem. Eric had refused to tell him his reasons for thinking a body might be in the creek, but he had begged the lieutenant to look. Ed Mitchell would have rather forgotten the whole thing, but he respected Eric, and the boy had been so urgent in his appeal he couldn't forget it.

Still, he would look pretty stupid if he got a crew out there and they dredged up nothing but old tires, and he couldn't even tell them why he was dragging it. Sam Burks, the editor of Ivy's daily newspaper would sure give it to him for that—cartoons and everything. To Sam Burks, everybody in public office was fair game, and police detectives were at the top of his list.

Besides, he thought, slumping down in the chair behind his desk, he didn't know how to drag a creek. He had never dragged one in his life. He was in larceny, not homicide. Maybe he should just turn it over to homicide and forget it. No, if Eric were wrong, that would look bad for both of them. He would have to drag the creek himself. But he didn't have any drag hooks.

He almost wished something important—like a bank robbery—would come up that would let him forget Eric's call. He wondered whether Alison knew anything about it. Probably not. That wasn't the kind of thing Eric would let her in on.

Sighing, he reached for the phone and dialed a number.

A voice answered. "Nick's Welding. Nick speaking."

"Hey, Nick," said Mitchell. "I need three or four big hooks. I wonder if you could weld me up some out of some three-eighths reinforcement rods."

"Sure. Where you figure on fishing with something like that, Ed? Ain't no whales around here this time of year." He chuckled kiddingly.

"These aren't fish hooks. I gotta look for something in the creek, and I figured I could drag it with something like that. What do you think?"

"Sure. I can make you up some. Four of 'em? About a foot-and-a-half-long, turned up about eight or ten inches?"

"That ought to do it."

"Whatcha looking for, anyway, Ed? Some dead bodies?" Nick laughed uproariously at his own joke.

"Yeah, or maybe a dead cow. Can I pick them up about ten o'clock?"

He recruited Mike Silvers, Jack Jackson, and Mort Sculley of his own department, and they rented a small boat with an outboard from Mike's uncle, who ran a small fishing and boating concession on the upper end of the creek. Nobody ever came down by the place where the planing mill was anymore. Nobody except people with junk to throw into the stream. Ed Mitchell figured they'd be pulling trash out of the water all day long with nothing to show for it. He had wished for a long time that the city would do something about the dumping.

He refused to tell his men what he was looking for. "I got a tip on the phone yesterday," he said. "I think it's phony; so I'm not going to tell you guys anything about it. Just keep throwing the harpoons in the water where I tell you, and we'll see what comes up. O.K.?''

"O.K." It was Mike's day off, and he wasn't happy. He had figured on getting some baseball practice that morning. He was star shortstop of the Ivy Rooters, but there were a couple of new kids coming up that were pretty good, too, and every time he missed practice, he was afraid he'd come back and find one of them in his place.

Jack and Mort were fishermen. They asked Ed if they could bring their poles along. He yelled back at them with the anger of which he was sometimes capable, "This is a business trip, you meatheads!"

They picked up the hooks from Nick and got their boat and ropes together and got onto the water about ten-thirty. They put in at a small beach upstream. They got the gear aboard the boat and started the motor. In a few minutes, they were down at the deep hole off the clay point.

Their first and second hauls were old tires.

"And this was one of the best fishing holes any-where," said Mort in disgust.

"People lack respect anymore," said Jack.

They pulled up a rusty bedspring.

For an hour or more they moved slowly back and forth across the stream. The sun was getting hot on their backs and reflected from the water's surface in blinding radiance. The three recruits became tired and disgusted with the fruitless task, whose purpose they didn't even know.

"Can't we knock it off until it gets cooler?" said Jack.

"It'd at least be more fun if we knew what we were looking for," said Mike.

Ed Mitchell was torn between his own frustration and his feeling he should give Eric's request a chance.

*"Maybe right close to the bank, as if it had rolled down from the point," Eric had said. We haven't really got that close in,* the lieutenant thought.

"Let's try once more back up where we started, only closer in to the bank," he said. "I think we missed a spot there."

Mike turned the boat around with mock weariness and headed toward the clay bank. He stopped the engine. Ed Mitchell looked up.

"Looks like something might have slid down there recently, doesn't it?" said the detective. "And look at that spot in the grass over there. A big, square rock might have been sitting there until not too long ago. But you don't see the rock anywhere around now."

"Somebody slid it into the water just for kicks," said Jack.

"Yeah—" said Ed Mitchell. "Let's see if we can find it."

They cast the hooks again and moved the boat slowly downstream. Another tire and a piece of rusty auto frame.

Ed gathered in the rope and slung the hook up the bank, letting it fall down the slope into the water. He gave a tug. It held.

"Guess what, fellas," said Jack. "Lay you two to one it's an old baby carriage."

"Model A Ford body," said Mike.

"Forget it you guys," said Mort. "Pull it in and let's get going."

There was a strangeness in the feel of what the hook had snagged. Ed Mitchell straightened up. He felt a vague apprehension. "Give a hand," he said in a quiet voice. "But take it easy—real easy—not too fast there—"

Mike gave a sudden exclamation of horror and fell back in the boat. Jack and Mort seemed frozen as they gazed into the water.

"Pull real easy," said Ed Mitchell. He had seen it, too, and his strong stomach felt as if it were going to give up whatever was inside.

# 13 • Disturbing News

The girls had got up early that morning. They showered and dressed, and Alison Two brushed her hair the way Alison One had shown her. She was proud of her hair now. It looked just like Alison's, thick and dark.

She studied her face in the mirror. It had been less than three weeks since she had moved into the Thornes' house; yet she had aged at least a full year.

At that time, Alison stepped into the room. "Something wrong?" she asked.

"Yes," the clone replied sadly, still facing the mirror. "It's happening. It's happening just as Three said, just as Professor Swykert had told us. I'm aging faster every day. I see every day how much older my face looks. I *feel* it—inside me."

"But you don't—"

"Please, Alison. Don't hold back anything from me. I can take it. I just want you to be honest with me."

"All right." Alison smiled sadly. "I promise."

Alison Two suddenly whirled about, her face bright. "I just thought of something nice. Let's go on a picnic today. You and me. Just the two of us."

"A picnic?"

"I've never been on a picnic. But I read in a book once about some people who went on one, and it sounded like so much fun. Is there a place where we could go on a picnic?"

"Lots of places along the creek. People picnic there all the time. It sounds like a wonderful idea! Let's get a basket of lunch together and go right away. I know just the place!"

The spot Alison chose was a familiar one. She had attended countless church and school picnics there. It was a small, sandy beach a few hundred feet long. Back from the water a way, it was still grassy under the shade of giant poplars. Alison and her friends had often gone there on summer evenings to watch the ripple of the water in the moonlight and listen to the quiet sounds.

Alison parked in the shade. The girls had worn bathing suits under slacks and blouses. They put the styrofoam cooler containing their lunch down on the grass and spread out the blanket they had packed.

"Let's swim, first," said Alison.

"I'll go in the water with you. But I don't know how to swim," said Alison Two.

"It's mostly for wading, anyway, along here. There aren't many places deep enough to swim until you get way out." Alison began removing her slacks. "Come on. I'll race you down to the water!"

They raced over the grass to the sand and into the water. It was cold and fresh.

Alison had brought a big beach ball, and they tossed it about and splashed one another and screamed at the cold splash of water on their faces. Finally, their arms about one another, they tried to duck each other and succeeded and came up laughing and squealing and ran back up the beach to flop on the blankets and dry off in the warm sun.

Alison Two lay on her face, her head cushioned on her arms. She was quiet, but her shoulders moved faintly. Alison thought for a moment she might be crying and moved to touch her, but she raised her head suddenly and there was such gladness in her face that Alison moved back so as not to disturb it.

"Oh, I've never, *never* done anything so wonderful!" cried Alison Two. "The air, the grass, the sand, the water—I didn't know anything could be so wonderful."

She turned over and looked up at Alison. "You've known these things all your life, haven't you?" she said.

Alison nodded. "Yes. The world is a pretty wonderful place."

"You've known it for years, for a lifetime." Alison Two's voice was suddenly tiny. "I get to know it for a day—"

There was nothing Alison could say.

Alison Two faced her again. "You've had boy-friends, too?"

175

"Yes. I know a lot of nice boys."

"I wish I could have known a boyfriend." Alison Two bit her lip and hit her hand against the ground. "You'll get married, too, someday, won't you?"

"I expect to."

"And you'll have children—and they'll have children—and it will go on forever. Look at me!" she exploded in bitterness now. "I never had a mother. I'll never have a child. When I'm gone, it will be as if I never were!"

Alison put her arms around Alison Two and held her now and rocked her back and forth like a child. "Alison, my Alison—don't you know I'm your mother. The cells of my body are the cells of your body. You came into being out of me. I'm your mother just as much as if I'd given you birth. Alison, my daughter, my child—"

They rocked back and forth, and the summer breeze blew over them and a few leaves trickled through the air and fell upon them.

Alison Two straightened after a time and sat up, away from Alison. She looked up at the heights of the trees and the sky. Her eyes came back to Alison's.

"Tell me about God," she said. "Am I His child, too? Or am I just a—nothing. Like this wind that blows about us, and then is gone. Is that all I am?"

"God is the reason we are here," Alison began. "God created all this beautiful world for us to enjoy. He created us—both you and me—to love us and for us to love Him. It is God who gives us life. Dr. Swykert had learned many of the mysteries of life, but its source is

176

always God. God has put you here, just as He has put me here."

They remained on the picnic ground until afternoon, talking of God and life and love. The more they talked, the happier they became. They ate their lunch of cold chicken and potato salad and pop. They lay on the pillows and watched the white clouds sailing over, heading southwest. They had a contest, finding puppy dogs, and elephants, and fantastic animals with no name, in the white cloud masses traveling far above.

"Oh, I love this world!" Alison Two said again.

"I love it, too. I guess I really didn't know how much until you showed me. You have really taught me to appreciate what God has given me."

When they were about ready to leave, they saw a pickup truck with a boat and other gear passing slowly on the creek road beyond the picnic ground. Alison recognized Lt. Mitchell. She waved to him.

The lieutenant was driving. He waved back. The truck slowed, seemed to hesitate, and then stopped.

"Duck behind that tree and pick some flowers," Alison quickly told Alison Two. "Keep your head down."

The lieutenant got out and came toward the girls. He walked slower than usual, Alison thought. She wondered why he had stopped at all.

As he approached he said, "Hello, Alison. I didn't know whether to stop or not. It doesn't really concern you, and yet it does, in a way."

"What is it?"

"That fellow that robbed Sam Barrett's store—and

who we thought for a while was Eric—we just found his body in the creek down by the planing mill. I thought maybe you'd like to know so you wouldn't be worrying any more about him showing up and being mistaken for Eric."

Alison tried to keep from showing any sign of the panic that gripped her. Alison Two froze under the tree.

"Eric will be relieved to hear that," Alison said.

"It was Eric who put me onto it. He called me last night."

"Eric's in Arabia!"

"He told me he was in Egypt. That's where he called me from. He asked me to drag the creek. He seemed to know where we'd find a body. I got to call him and let him know. I guess he just got to thinking about it and figured, for some reason, that's what happened. I'll have to ask him. Anyway, the fellow must have been sleeping on the bank and somebody stabbed him and robbed him. Anything you want me to tell Eric?"

"No." Alison shook her head and tried to keep her jaw from trembling. "Nothing I can think of. Just tell him hello and that we're waiting for him to get back."

"Another funny thing: Whoever did it took all this fellow's clothes and put a rock in them and threw them in the creek, too. All he had on when we found him was a wrist watch."

Alison Two suppressed a gasp.

"Oh?" said Alison. "We might have seen that watch when we talked to him in Midland. What kind was it?"

"Gold-colored. Digital type, Plastic, imitation alligator band. We'll hold it for evidence. It might be our only clue to his identity." He turned away. "Well, I hope I haven't upset you by telling you this, but I thought maybe you ought to know because of the mix-up about his looking like Eric. I'll give Eric your regards."

The lieutenant strode away, and Alison Two rejoined Alison.

Alison said, "That night Three went out of the house for a walk—Two was waiting and killed him. He took Three's clothes and came to our house and told us he had fallen into the water."

Alison Two was trembling so hard she couldn't stop. "Two killed my brother—he was a real brother. He was the only family I ever had."

Alison stared across the distant prairie. "And now he's with my brother in Egypt. It's not Three who's with Eric. It's Two, and he's a murderer."

# 14 • Escape Attempt

Still in his Sessim disguise, Eric slept uneasily through the night. He half expected attack from some quarter; he didn't know what.

He was awakened at last by the sound of Two's moving about next door, showering and whistling. Eric wondered what they would do during the day. It turned out they did nothing. Except wait fruitlessly.

Eric debated with himself whether or not he should go back and make contact at the final station he was supposed to have delivered the package to. Maybe Holcomb was still waiting for a report of his arrival there. Otherwise, the agent might not know what had become of Eric. The more he thought of it, the more he berated himself for not going there rather than high-tailing it back to the hotel. But now he had to wait. He had to talk to Ed Mitchell again.

To be sure.

They read in their rooms. The clone seemed more at

ease and resigned to waiting than before, Eric thought. He seemed almost cheerful. They had lunch together and took separate walks in the afternoon. When he was alone, Eric tried to call the number by which he had reached Holcomb before. He tried a half dozen times. There was never any answer or any indication the phone was out of service. It rang, but no one answered.

They ate dinner together at about eight-thirty. The clone didn't seem hungry and finished his meal quickly. Eric dawdled.

"I'll leave you with it, if you don't mind," said Two. "I'm going up and do some more studying. I've hit something rather interesting."

"Fine," said Eric. "I'll be along after a while."

He gave the clone time to reach the room. Then he put in a call again to Mitchell. The operator told him there was a half-hour wait. It was nearly an hour. But he finally got through. The lieutenant answered immediately.

"Just got in." His voice sounded exhausted. "We found what you figured we'd find. I want to know how you knew. We've got to find out who did it. This is a murder!"

For a moment, Eric couldn't talk. He found his hand shaking so much he could scarcely hold the phone. He had known what the answer would be, but he just hadn't wanted to believe it. He looked around apprehensively.

"Eric?"

"It's a long story, Mr. Mitchell, and I can't possibly

tell all of it to you now. I'll tell you everything I know when I get back—which will be soon."

"Eric, it's not just me. Homicide is in on this now. You—"

"Lieutenant, I just don't *know* anything that will help you. I appreciate your doing what I asked, and I'll make it up to you in any way I can."

"All right," said Ed Mitchell grudgingly. "I'll be looking for you soon. By the way, we ran into Alison on the way. I told her about it. I don't know whether I should. It seemed to upset her, but I thought she had an interest in knowing since she was involved with this guy through Barrett's robbery and her going with you to Midland to see him."

Eric groaned to himself, but said nothing to the detective about such idiocy. "There's one thing I'd appreciate your doing: Call Alison. Tell her you've talked to me and that I'm O.K. Also tell her to try to get a line to Jim Holcomb through his office and tell him I need to talk to him. She'll know what I mean. But be sure to tell her everything is all right with me."

"Sure, Eric, but—"

"I've got to hang up now, Mr. Mitchell. Please believe me. I'll do everything I can to help you on this case."

He hung up before Ed Mitchell could protest again.

He leaned against the wall of the partition and put the phone to his face again. He didn't want to go out for a minute. He couldn't seem to breathe.

He hadn't wanted to believe.

Now he had to. There was no other answer.

He saw how it could have happened. Two had never left town that night he fled from Swykert's place. He had hung around, hoping somehow to catch Three alone. And it had probably been much easier than he had ever hoped. By deciding to go out for a stroll that first night, Three had walked right into his arms. Somewhere in the dark. Maybe down by the creek. Maybe somewhere else. That didn't matter. Two had caught Three, killed him, and dumped him in the creek after taking his clothes. Then he had gone to the Thornes', pretending to be Three and giving the story of having fallen into the creek.

And now he was traveling with Eric, under the protection of the CIA, wide open to contact whatever enemy agents he could find to accept his gift of the deadly EMR weapon.

Obviously, he had made such contact. He had turned over his work, and the enemy was trying to get it out of Egypt. Jim Holcomb had spotted them and had tried to use Eric to intercept.

And he had fouled it up completely. He hadn't trusted Holcomb and had bungled the trap that Holcomb must have laid with meticulous care.

Yet, he didn't understand why Holcomb didn't just walk in on Two and take him in custody.

He should have trusted Holcomb.

He *had* to trust him now.

But he didn't know how to reach him.

As for Two—if the clone had the slightest suspicion

185

that he had been detected, there would be yet another murder.

Eric's.

He couldn't go back to the room. There was absolutely no way he could do that. He couldn't spend another night in a room next to the murderous clone.

He checked his pockets. He had his wallet with his travel funds, his identification as Mr. Sessim, and the keys to Hassam's old car. That was all. It had to be enough.

He glanced carefully about and stepped away from the phone. He saw no sign of Two. He passed through the back of the lobby and into the parking lot, which was well lighted. The old Chevy was parked in plain view of the windows of Two's room. He had to chance it.

He stepped out and ran for the car. It started easily, and Eric gave thanks for Hassam's excellent mechanic, whoever he might be. He drove a route that gave him least exposure to observation from the windows above. Then he turned into the street along the opposite side of the hotel.

His most immediate chance of locating Holcomb was touching base with the station he had missed. Maybe it was a forlorn and hopeless chance now. But he could think of no other plan.

The highway south along the Nile was crowded somewhat with evening traffic, but it thinned as he passed the outskirts of the city. He drove as fast as he dared. The city's haze of light fell behind, and the clear atmosphere of the desert opened the wonders of the southern sky to him.

The edge of the great city melted into the farmlands and villages that clutched the lifeline of the Nile as it meandered from the center of Africa. Traffic became less and less. Only a trickle of cars came from the south. A few scattered lights from behind bobbed in his rear-view mirror.

He tried not to think of the unreality of his situation—fleeing through the desert of Egypt away from a fantastic creature created in the laboratory of a madman. That's how he thought of Swykert now. Like the fabled Dr. Frankenstein, Swykert had created a monster who had the intent and the ability to destroy the world. Yes, there had been Three, and there was Alison Two, and their goodness was not to be denied. But Swykert's monster was his monument.

Eric was annoyed by a pair of too-bright lights in his mirror. They were far back, but they were powerful. He flipped the mirror to divert the reflection away from his eyes.

In his mind, he checked the image of the map of the countryside. The place he was looking for was about sixty miles from Cairo. He reached his turn-off in a little over an hour. The side road was sandy and rough, leading into clusters of distant farm villages. He slowed to less than thirty-five.

After a few minutes of driving on the farm road, his attention was attracted by an image in his outside mirror. The strong headlights that had been behind him almost all the way from Cairo had made the turn, too. He adjusted the inside mirror back. There was no mistaking. The other car was following him.

He didn't want to believe it. It was a coincidence. He stepped on the gas and gripped the wheel more firmly. The car behind accelerated, too.

And more than enough to keep up with him. It was slowly closing the gap between them now, less than a mile behind. He pressed the gas pedal to the floor. It was almost impossible to keep the car on the road with the violent jolting.

Eric assumed that Two was in the car behind with whoever his contact was—or one of the contact's agents, at least. Two would not be driving.

It was obvious the powerful car could close on the Chevy any time the driver wanted to. Eric glanced from side to side. He knew that in the darkness, tall wheatfields lay on either side of the road. He was glad the Egyptian farmers were a little late with their harvesting. He took a good look at the road ahead to fix it in his memory. Then he switched off the lights.

He continued driving at top speed for the length of road he could recall. Then he cut the engine and slammed on the emergency brake. As the car skidded to a halt, he opened the door and rolled out. He landed painfully on his left shoulder, sliding and rolling in the stifling sand and dust of the road.

As soon as he stopped rolling, he scrambled to his feet and crawled around the front of his car to avoid the glow of the pursuing lights. He dived into the dry ditch

188

at the edge of the field and plunged into the tall stand of wheat.

Keeping his arms outstretched like the prow of a boat, he bored his way through the dry stalks. Dust rose about him, half suffocating. He stumbled and fell headlong, the sharp, broken stalks stabbing through his shirt. He got to his knees and glimpsed the light of the pursuing car as it reached his own abandoned car and stopped. The lights were cut off abruptly, as if the pursuers were trying to adjust their eyes to the darkness. Eric's were already used to it, and he was able to recognize the car as a dark-colored Mercedes. Three men got out of it. Moments later, the beam of a flashlight began to play about.

He turned to his left and plunged ahead. After a hundred yards, he came to a ditch and fell again. He gasped with pain as his knee hit the opposite bank. Desperately, he got to his feet and continued on. Then he backtracked the way he had come and returned to the ditch. There, he hunched down and ran along the bottom of the shallow depression, keeping his head below the level of the wheat.

Once, he stopped and looked up cautiously. The flashlight beam was playing about in the wheat a few yards from the road, as if his pursuers were trying to track his path through the field. It would not be hard in daylight, but the darkness slowed them down, even with the flashlight. They were far behind him and not gaining.

He began to breathe easier. If he could keep out of

their reach until morning, perhaps he could find safety in the village that had been his goal another three miles down the farm road.

He sat on the edge of the ditch, concealed below the wheat, to take a few moments of rest. Then he tensed, like a pointer that suddenly had the quarry. The scent of smoke was drifting in the air. He stood up and turned toward the road. A small yellow flickering light shone in the darkness back by the cars. Then another—

They were firing the wheatfield.

He heard the crackle of dry straw as the flames bit into it. The smoke intensified, borne on the fair wind that blew toward him.

Eric stared in despair. There was no way he could outrun the flames. But he had to try. The yellow tongues leaped in the air, surging eagerly forward like bright hounds in the night. He watched the ditch stretching ahead of him. Not trying to keep his head down now—he figured the smoke and flames would shield him from his enemies—he ran with all his strength and speed along the center of the ditch to put as much distance as he possibly could between him and the road.

It was only minutes, however, until he felt the heat of the fire behind him. His lungs felt about to burst, and he gave up his running. He plunged into the bottom of the ditch. With his fingers, he scratched at the thin crust over the moist soil beneath. It was the silt of the Nile, which had given life to the valley for centuries as it overflowed each season and spread its fertile deposits over the desert sands. Now, with the dam far up the river's course, this nourishment was gone, but what had been laid down centuries ago remained.

He dug into it. A foxhole. He made it as deep as possible and lay face down, full length. He scratched the soil back over himself as best as he could. He drew his shirt up over his head and lay with his face in his arms.

He prepared for inferno.

# 15 • Big Night Ahead

The holocaust came quickly. Not only the wind of the night, but the blast of heated air from the exploding straw. It roared like a blowtorch and brought with it the smoke. He pressed his palms against his eyes. He filtered the air through his shirt and the little mound of moist soil he had accumulated under his face. *Dear Lord,* he prayed, *please see me through this!*

It got worse. The flames grew to a miniature firestorm that totally consumed the oxygen of the air and left only dead gases for him to breathe. He gasped and tried to suck air through his mouth. He got only smoke and remnants of air without oxygen. He choked and smothered as these waste gases collected around him like a soft, fiery pillow.

The flames came then in full fury. Like the tongues of hungry, yellow mastiffs, they licked at him, burned his shirt from his back, and scorched his skin.

It would be over in a minute, he kept telling himself.

The flames would burn themselves out and move on. It couldn't last. He could see it through—

But before he did, consciousness left him as the smoke filled his lungs and the last of his oxygen was exhausted.

He heard dogs yelping, and he raised his head, an action which cost him unbelievable agony. Face down again on his arms, he remembered faintly from that one ghastly attempt to come alive that the yellow fire glow was gone, and there seemed to be a touch of dawn in the sky. He tried again. It was a little less agonizing, and the dawn's glow was actually there.

He became aware of his back. It was one mass of pain. He rested on his arms while he endured the pain and willed it to go away. It didn't. Still, he was grateful to be alive, and he thanked God.

Then he struggled to his knees and raised his head. He was face to face with the leanest, meanest, and biggest dog he had ever seen in his life. Gray, like a ghost.

The dog looked him over, its jowls dripping; then it turned and loped away. In a moment, it returned, yelping fiercely but looking back over its shoulder rather than at Eric.

He heard voices, jangling, excited, urgent voices in some Egyptian dialect he did not understand, but he got the idea the men were quite excited and satisfied to find him.

Friends or enemies? He had no friends out here.

They lifted him carefully and stood him on his feet. Their mahogany faces looked grave and sympathetic. They looked exhausted, as if they had been up all night. One of them gestured to a stretcher carried by another man. Eric shook his head and took a step on his own. He would have collapsed if they had not caught him.

He submitted to the stretcher.

Slowly they carried him out of the smoking field the way he had come. They passed his car. It had been set afire, too, and now only blackened framework remained. Eric noted this with regret. He had become fond of Hassam's ancient car.

His attackers' car was gone.

It was evident the men he was with were ones who had fought the fire all night until they had beaten it. But it had consumed tens of acres of their wheat crop. That would be their year's supply of grain, Eric thought. Because of him, they would go hungry.

In apprehension, he turned to see their faces. What would they do with him? There was no sign of animosity he could detect. They carried him carefully and tenderly, and they were headed down the road to the village of his final station, three miles away.

He must hage dozed or lapsed into unconsciousness. The next thing he knew, he was in a house, an adobe hut like all those he was familiar with in these villages. They were shifting him carefully from the stretcher onto the straw mat that he knew was the bed of the man and wife of the house. A moment later, three of the women

194

who came from some other rooms were lightly rinsing his back, after which they rubbed it gently with soothing oil. He had no idea what it was, but it felt good. He dozed off again.

When he revived once more, he did not know where he was. He sat up with a start, thinking he was back in his room at the Nile Hilton and that Two had done something horrible to him. Then he saw the young Egyptian sitting on the floor three feet from the mat, and he remembered and slumped down on his side.

The Egyptian spoke in quite good English. "You are feeling better, sir?"

"Much better." He shifted his position. The pain was miraculously much less. "I guess I have you to thank—and others of your family, and your neighbors. I am grateful."

"We are happy to have helped. My father would have been pleased, I think, with our efforts."

Eric caught a note of enveloping sadness in the man's voice and became aware that the Egyptian had griefs of his own. Eric glanced about the room. There were others he had not noticed before. An older woman and a young girl watched him like mourners from near the door. Three men in their thirties were grouped at the head of the mat on which he lay. They all watched but left the speaking to the man who sat on the floor nearby.

"The fire—it burned your fields," said Eric.

The young man nodded. "We saved much. Our neighbors will share." His expression did not change. He might have been reporting the weather.

Eric looked around once more at all the grave, immobile faces. "Something else has happened!" he exclaimed. "Tell me what they did to you!"

The man seemed ready to tell, as if he had been waiting for Eric to give him his cue. "They came in the middle of the night," he said, "while our fields were burning and we were getting ready to go fight the fire. They demanded the radio, and my father said there was no radio. They told him they would shoot him if he did not bring it to them. He said there was no radio, and they shot him. He lies in the room beyond. We shall bury him today."

Eric's vision clouded as sudden grief filled him. He wanted to shout: "Swykert, your monster is loose! Your great gift to the world, Dr. Swykert!"

"I am sorry," he said weakly. "I brought them upon you."

"No." The young Egyptian shook his head. "Men like these are everywhere. You do not bring them. We bring them on ourselves, and you help us fight them. We are grateful to you."

Eric knew he must say no more. There was no more to be said to these people, who regarded *him* as their supporter and helper.

He had been catching glimpses of the smashed debris in the corner of the room behind the man who spoke.

"That—" He pointed. "The radio?"

"They held my wife, Ashira, next." He gestured to the younger woman by the door. "And then my mother. I knew they would also be killed. I had to bring them the

196

radio. They stomped on it and left. We went to fight the fire."

The faces about him remained impassive, but not accusing. He had brought them tragedy, and they did not blame him. In the doorway, the big gray dog that had found him sank on its haunches and regarded him with much the same expression as the Egyptians.

Eric sat up painfully. *Where to, next?* he wondered. *Two is still on the loose, with the support and protection now of one or more enemy agents. And I have no place to go. Two undoubtedly thinks I died in the fire. That, at least, means he won't be following. But where to, next?*

The young Egyptian moved as Eric sat up. "We have time for a meal. Then Mr. Jim will be here."

Eric jerked his head about with a start. "Mr. Who?"

"Mr. Jim. Mr. Holcomb. He said he would be here by the hour after the meal."

"How do you know that? How could Jim Holcomb tell you anything?" He glanced toward the smashed remains in the far corner.

"The other radio. We always have another one. But my father was a stubborn man. He spit in their faces. He would give them nothing."

Eric sank back in disbelief. But there was no way they could know the name of Jim Holcomb unless it was all for real.

"You called Mr. Holcomb after the men were gone?"

"Yes. He had been calling for you since you had not arrived two days ago. We told him what had happened after the men had gone. And when we found you, we called again and said we believed we had his messenger. We described you, and he said we were right, and he would be here as soon as possible, but that would not be until after meal time. Will you eat with us now, Mr. Thorne?"

Another shock. Holcomb must have used his correct name to them. He let it go and nodded assent. He would be glad to eat. He was very hungry. It would be an honor.

Jim Holcomb arrived on time, just at the conclusion of the meal. He looked far different than he had in Ivy. He no longer resembled the enthusiastic high-school science teacher that Eric once saw in him. He looked exhausted and dirty. His beard was days old. His face bore the mark of the desert in its parched lines. He looked *tough*.

He was offered food, which he accepted, but he seemed to be in a great hurry. He had scarcely finished when he arose from the cushion on which he sat. "We have very little time," he said to Eric. "We have to go."

The Egyptian family gathered to bid them goodbye as if they were beloved kin whom they had not seen for a long time. Holcomb pressed some money into the hand of the young man. "For the burned wheat," he said. It was accepted gratefully.

The giant gray dog—Eric had learned his name was Dinbar—stood by the family in the doorway as Holcomb turned his car around. The Egyptians were left to the grim task of burying their stubborn father—who had spit in the face of his enemies when they threatened him.

"We can't go back to your hotel," Holcomb said. "It will be watched."

They passed the burned wheat field, and the smell of smoke was still in the air. Eric could feel himself lying again in the ditch with the roaring tigers of fire leaping about him.

Jim Holcomb caught his glance. "I'm sorry you were placed at such risk. It was not intended. We meant to get you out if you were spotted. Some things went wrong. You didn't show up at Akim's, and we didn't catch what had happened."

They passed Hassam's burned-out car. "Who will be watching?" said Eric. "I want to know what's happening. I feel I've been a piece in a chess game, and I've been pushed around without knowing where I was going."

"You have," said Holcomb. "We needed you, and we used you. I think, in time, you will forgive us."

"I'd like to know the whole story. I discovered that Two killed Three back in Ivy, and I've been traveling ever since with a murderer—one who would have willingly finished me off if he guessed I knew his secret. That's what he tried to do by burning the wheat field."

"I knew," said Holcomb. "I knew from what I saw in your house that night I came to visit you. I knew from the way he acted and from the bruises on his face. You remember I told you that in my business some of us learn to smell a lie. Well, that night I smelled his lies.

"In addition, there was the damage to his clothes, which I took a look at down in the laundry room. That damage didn't come from a slide into the creek. He had been in a fight. Three must have put up a terrible struggle for his life. I don't know just how he was killed. You've talked with the Ivy Police? They found the body and called you? Did they say anything about a weapon?"

"I called *them,*" said Eric. "I found out that it was Two who was with me as a result of that package that was blown up at the pyramid. Some bits of paper were identical with the paper Two had in his room. His writing, his mathematical symbols, were on the paper in the package. Then I called Lt. Mitchell and got him to find Three's body in the creek."

"I see," said Holcomb. "That's where it all went wrong. And that's the reason you didn't make the last station—because you decided it was no good since you had nothing to deliver."

"That's right. Something spooked the courier and he destructed the package. Then I found out that it was Two who was with me, and I *really* needed you. The only thing I could think of was to go to the final station after all. That's when Two and his buddies tried to get me."

"It was our mistake," Holcomb acknowledged. "We sidetracked the real courier, whose place you took, but we didn't get all the signal. You were supposed to give the other courier another signal before you took the second picture. When he didn't get it, he let the package blow and ran.''

"It was a courier network to get Two's EMR weapon data to Russia?"

"Yes. We knew the channels that would be used. We had a ready line of interception set up. We thought we could use you in that line, but we did not intend the risk to which we exposed you. Of course, some risk existed the moment you left Ivy with Two, but that risk *had* to be taken if we were to expose him. There was absolutely no way out."

They came onto the main road and joined the stream of traffic heading for Cairo. Holcomb handled the big car with a light touch. Eric realized it was specially built. He felt the power of an engine such as cars had back in the sixties. The console in front of him resembled the panel of a jet aircraft.

"So you knew all the time that I was traveling with Two," said Eric. "And you say it was necessary. I don't understand that. Why didn't you just grab him and be done with it?"

"On what basis? We could never have proved in court that he killed Three. If we had tried talking to a judge and jury about Swykert and clones, we'd have been thrown completely out. Two would have been turned loose by any court."

"And now he's loose anyway. What is there to get him on now?"

Holcomb's hands gripped the wheel a shade tighter.

He watched the road ahead and the skyline of Cairo for several seconds before he answered.

He said, "You called Two the most dangerous man in the world. Do you still believe that?"

"Yes," said Eric. "I believe it on the basis of what Three told me. I believe what Three said when he told me Two had a weapon and the desire to destroy mankind from the face of the earth. And I heard Two repeat that desire."

"I believe it, too," said Holcomb. "I believed it the moment I first saw Two—even before you told me about him. I *knew* in your house that night that he was the person you were speaking of. I've been around evil men all my career, and I've learned that when a man wants to kill and destroy, you can feel it if you open your senses. Most people keep their senses closed to such feelings; they're too painful to confront. It's my business to confront them."

Eric remembered his desperate refusal to believe his companion was actually Two until Lt. Mitchell confirmed it.

"I think I know what you mean. I didn't want to believe he was Two."

"We couldn't just give him a traffic ticket and tell him to watch himself from now on," said Holcomb. "We had to *nail* him—once and for all, and it had to be on a basis of something *big*. To do that, we had to get him out of the country. Do you begin to understand now?"

Eric stared at the Cairo skyline and nodded. He felt a fierce tightening in his stomach as he realized the role he had played up to now. "The pretended chase around the world after an imaginary Two was your way of getting him into a position where you could nail him."

"Yes. So you see, we're not through with him yet. We have maneuvered him into the position we want. Now we have a good night's work ahead of us."

Nearing the city, Holcomb took a road that wound around it on the outskirts. There, a quarter of the way around in a dilapidated section of the Old City, he stopped at a rundown hotel. "We'll take a break here," he said.

The sleepy innkeeper brushed the flies off the register and presented it to them. Holcomb registered as William Canning. He turned the book to Eric. "Here you go, Mr. Sessim," he said.

The clerk jerked a thumb toward the worn stairs behind him. "Top stairs," he said in battered English. "Last room. Right side."

Dust filtered down from the door casing as they pushed the door open. The room had not been used for many months.

Holcomb wearily threw his coat on the dusty chair and tried the shower in the bathroom. It delivered a small trickle.

"You go first," he said to Eric. "Leave that dressing on your back. After you shower, I'll change the dressing and put on some more of that dope he gave me."

"I hope it isn't goat manure and grasshopper juice," said Eric. "It was terrific the way it worked. My back feels almost well."

"Then don't worry about what's in it."

Eric undressed and showered carefully, and Holcomb redressed his burn.

"You're lucky it's not deep," said Holcomb. "It should be all right in a few days."

Holcomb took his turn in the feeble shower. He would have used a razor if one had been available, but he had nothing except the clothes he wore. Eric didn't ask where he'd been.

It was late afternoon when they finished. Eric sat in the one large chair—sideways a bit to favor his back. Holcomb lay on the bed, his eyes shut.

"I trust you won't be hungry for dinner," said Holcomb.

"Akim put on a pretty good feed, although it's still hard to get used to goat chops. It'll hold me. Where do we go from here?"

Holcomb didn't speak for quite a while. He lay with his arm over his eyes, and Eric thought he had gone to sleep. But then he spoke. "We should have a busy evening."

"Am I included?"

"I'd like you to see the finish. Hopefully, it *will* be a finish."

Eric waited. Holcomb volunteered no more.

"It might help if I had a little briefing," Eric said finally.

"Petrark," said Holcomb. "I don't suppose Two made any mention of Petrark to you, did he?"

"No."

Holcomb kept his arm over his eyes as he spoke. "Anton Petrark is the target we started out to get. We've had a network out for him for a long time. We were just about to close it when you came along with your story and the news of the EMR weapon Two was said to have developed. Petrark was big game. Two and his weapon were even bigger. It seemed natural to combine the hunt for both. We decided to have them meet."

"I didn't know Two had met anyone since we left Ivy."

"You weren't supposed to know. Two didn't want you to know. Neither did we."

"I get the uncomfortable feeling I've been used—by both sides," said Eric with some hostility in his voice.

Holcomb did not seem to notice the hostility. "Very usefully, too. You were of enormous help. In order to allow Two and Petrark to meet, we had to divert you. That's why we sent you to London for a couple of days."

"Then that nonsense—"

"It was an extremely important and useful action. It left Two alone here in Cairo for two days just after his arrival, and Petrark immediately made contact."

"What for? And who is Petrark, anyway?"

"He poses as a Turk, but he's actually a Russian agent. One of their best. He notes the arrival of Western technicians, or people who look like they might be technicians, and strikes up an acquaintance. He suggests that they might have information that would be

205

useful to a poor, developing country, information usually banned by secrecy laws and trade regulations. Almost every young engineer or scientist who comes over here carries something of the sort in his head. Much of it is useless junk. Some of it is very valuable. Petrark is authorized to pay sizable sums for information the Soviets might be able to use. He's been quite successful. So much so that we were given orders to cut him off—permanently. At any rate, he found Two immediately. And Petrark was exactly the kind of person Two was looking for. They fitted perfectly."

"I don't see why it would have been so hard to keep new arrivals from meeting Petrark," said Eric.

"We did that, partially, but he was still running around stirring up mischief wherever he could. As with Two, giving out parking tickets was no good. We had to nail him and all his elaborate apparatus for transferring illegal data to Russia. We had to break it all up. Your problem with Two helped make it possible."

"You took a big risk. Two and Petrark are together this minute, I assume. Two undoubtedly has a copy of his manuscript."

"As I said," Holcomb added, not moving on the bed, "tonight is going to be a big one."

"What do we do?"

# 16 • The Trap

It was nine P.M. when they left the hotel. Holcomb drove slowly through the evening traffic of Cairo and explained their plan.

"The manuscript is in Petrark's house—somewhere. Two is there with him. We could break in, but we might search for days before we found it, if at all. It would be impossible to break Petrark. I don't know about Two. At any rate, there's a much easier way to drive it out of hiding—and them, too."

"What?"

"The same thing they used on you. We're going to fire Petrark's house."

His agents were in place now, Holcomb explained. Petrark's own guards had been neutralized. It was known that Petrark had a plane standing by at the airport and planned to ferry the manuscript through Afghanistan and across the border into Russia, since his other courier network had been broken into.

"There must be an easier way," said Eric.

"He has to stay at arm's length from the Soviet Embassy," said Holcomb. "They won't have anything to do with him. Otherwise, he could use regular diplomatic pouch. But they know if he's caught and shows any connection with them, the Embassy would be ordered out of the country. They can't afford that. This is too valuable a listening post for them.

"Regular mail channels are out, too, of course. They're unreliable and censored to boot. Petrark's kind of information is for very special eyes in Moscow only. He has to use underground channels of communication."

"So when is he planning to fly Two's EMR data out of here?"

"We don't know. He probably hasn't decided. But it doesn't matter. We're not going to let him get that far. That's why we're going to force his hand tonight. He won't care if his whole house burns down. The one thing he will certainly salvage will be the EMR package. He's convinced this could be the big coup of his career."

"So how do we capture it—and him—and Two?"

"We play it by ear when we get there."

Eric suspected there was more to it than that. It was certain that Holcomb had a very definite plan of action, but he didn't want to discuss it further.

Petrark occupied an estate in the richest and most fashionable part of Cairo. Five acres of grounds planted with lawns, exotic flowers, palms, and plane trees. A vast, white stucco house centered the grounds. Petrark's jewel, as he sometimes called it. He was very proud of his house, for it excelled the four-room apartment he had left behind long ago in Russia.

As an observation post, Holcomb's men had rented an apartment in a high-rise building a mile-and-a-half away. From there, the Petrark estate had been under close surveillance with powerful telescopes for a week.

Holcomb headed for the apartment building. He and Eric went directly to the elevator. They got out on the eleventh floor and stepped into a soundless corridor laid with thick, green and white flowered carpeting. They walked swiftly toward the east. Holcomb knew the way.

He gave a signal with his electronic beeper, and the door opened. Inside, the room was almost dark. Three men in shirtsleeves were present. By the window was the shadow of the light-amplification telescope trained on Petrark's estate. One of the men was observing the target scene. A speaker nearby revealed the buzz of sound on the grounds, gathered by the tele-mike.

Holcomb didn't bother to introduce Eric. He checked with the leader of the group. Eric heard their low voices.

Target's men have been neutralized and replaced by our own," said the group leader. He sounded to Eric as if he were a mission controller reporting the conditions for an impending space flight.

"The dogs have been taken out," he continued. "Munitions are in place. Target's car is in the drive, well away from the projected fire area."

"Target personnel?" said Holcomb.

"Both inside the house. A housekeeper and three men are also inside. We have a man assigned to each."

Holcomb glanced at his watch. "All right. We'll proceed according to schedule. Notify me of any change in conditions."

"Yes, sir."

They drove slowly toward the not-too-distant plain, where merchants, politicians, scoundrels, and speculators—anyone clever enough to amass the necessary wealth—had built monuments to themselves in rich estates that competed with each other for quiet luxury. The area was patrolled by private police, and suspicious strangers were questioned. Holcomb's men had made extensive preliminary preparations with these private officers. They were nowhere in sight this night.

Lights were on in most of the great house. A few quiet parties were in progress. Some of the dogs—most of the places employed a pair of mastiffs or police dogs to watch—were conversing in subdued barks. Small security lights glowed on posts in the grounds.

The quiet of the neighborhood gave Eric the sense of a deep, quiet river flowing with immense power, for here were houses of men of international power and wealth, whose daily actions rippled the markets and conference rooms of the world.

Holcomb continued slowly. He watched the dial of the precision chronometer in the console of the car. The hands touched eleven o'clock. Holcomb tightened his grip on the wheel expectantly. A quarter of a mile ahead a small puff of light appeared. Holcomb pressed the accelerator. The car darted forward.

Small incendiaries had been set at a dozen places in and about the house. They went off in one little burst after another, spreading their deadly light in broad circles. In a matter of seconds, yellow flames were clawing like tigers' paws at the stately mansion. Smoke swirled into the desert sky.

Holcomb let the car creep down the drive that led into the estate from the road. He stopped fifty feet behind the big, black Mercedes parked there. Scattered cries and hoarse shouts came from within the house. It wouldn't be long until a swarm of excited neighbors gathered about the fire, Eric thought. He was not aware that Holcomb's men had already set up a cordon to keep them back.

Holcomb gave a sudden hoarse exclamation and twisted his big bulk toward the door of the car. Two figures had darted from the exit at the side of the house and were rushing toward the Mercedes.

"Stay here!" Holcomb commanded quietly. "Count ten and turn on the lights."

He slipped out of the car. The swiftly moving pair came to the Mercedes, then, in consternation, approached Holcomb's car to see what was blocking the drive.

Eric switched on the lights. The two figures, momentarily blinded, put their hands to their eyes. One was Two. He carried a briefcase that Eric didn't recognize.

The other man had to be Petrark. Eric was astonished at the man's incredible bulk. His enormous middle rotated from side to side as he walked. He tried to peer beyond the blinding car lights. A gun was in his hand.

Eric heard the voice of Holcomb call out cheerfully. "A good job, Eric Thorne!" But he was not addressing Eric. He was calling to Two. "We've got him covered now. You can come this way. You'll get your pay for this!"

Both men looked startled for an instant. They hesitated in their dive to escape the lights. Petrark's face turned toward Two in astonishment. The words shouted by Holcomb rang in his ears. His face twisted with rage.

"Traitor!" he screamed. "Traitor!" He moved with incredible swiftness for his huge bulk and aimed the gun at Two. The clone tried to duck. Petrark's gun fired twice before Holcomb's gun spat silently out of the darkness. The fat Russian threw up his arms with a cry and slumped to the concrete of the drive.

Eric jumped from the car and ran to where Two fell. The clone was already dead. Eric felt a wave of horror as he looked down. He was glad Two was disguised; he wouldn't have wanted to see "his own" face in death.

*Could it have been any different?* he asked himself. *Could this wonderful creation of Swykert's have been saved?*

Holcomb was breaking open the locked briefcase that had fallen from Two's hand. He held out a sheaf of papers. "Is this the manuscript?" he demanded of Eric.

Eric fanned through the sheets the agent held. "They

are the ones I saw him writing in the hotel. It looks like the same material as on the scrap I picked up at the Pyramid. It has to be the EMR design."

Holcomb put the papers back in the briefcase; then he raced toward the blazing inferno of the house. He stood as close as possible and hurled the briefcase with all his strength into the center of the fire.

Eric watched the flames flare up to consume the case and its contents.

"The world will never know," he said.

"I hope not," said Holcomb. "I sincerely hope not."

Eric was ready to leave the next day. His disguise had been thoroughly removed, and when he looked into the mirror, he saw Eric Thorne. He was a little older, he thought. Something was gone from his face that used to be there when he was a young boy—and something was added. Maturity, he hoped.

And in the mirror, he saw the image of Holcomb sitting behind him in the chair on the far side of the room. The CIA Agent looked once more a little like a high-school science teacher. But different. He, too, seemed a bit older, as if he had seen something he had never known existed.

"The story of Dr. Frankenstein is no myth," Holcomb said. "We have had such men since the beginning of time. Men like Swykert, who think their great genius stands above every other consideration in the world. Swykert thought the world owed him great applause, and he was bitter because he hadn't received it in his lifetime. And all he did was loose a murderous monster. An ingenious, cleverly constructed monster, but a monster nevertheless."

"It might have been otherwise," said Eric. "Three—and Alison Two—"

Holcomb brushed aside his argument almost angrily. "He had no idea what he was doing. He didn't *care* what he was doing—except that it was something so exceptionally clever.

"Don't misunderstand me. Technology has a place in the world, but with it belongs responsibility. Genius without responsibility is like an idiot turned loose with a cannon.

"Today, there are corporations devoted to tinkering with the genes of life, the very building blocks of all organisms. They, too, are thinking of human clones. Someday they will try. They do their work for cleverness and money."

He jumped to his feet. "Excuse my soapbox, Eric. It's about time to go if you're going to catch your plane. I just want you to know I'll be forever grateful for your help in eradicating at least two of the monsters of the earth. Without you, we wouldn't have accomplished it. Now, the world is considerably better off."

Eric took one last look at his image in the mirror. *Two was me,* he thought, *just as Three was. Was Two the dark side of me, what I would have been had I never known the love of God?* He thanked God that he would never have to find out.

"I guess I've got everything," he said.

216

He arrived home the next day. He took a taxi from the airport rather than disturb Alison. When he walked in the front door, Aunt Rose was kneeling, polishing the floor of the entrance way.

"Watch what you're—" she started to scold. Then she looked up. "Eric Thorne! Land's sakes, boy, why don't you let people know when you're coming? Did you get to climb the pyramids while you were there?"

He returned her hug and patted her ample shoulder. "I saw a few," he said, "but I didn't climb any."

Over his aunt's shoulder, he saw Alison coming down the hall. She had never before looked quite so wonderful to him. "Hi, Sis," he said quietly.

She stopped and leaned against the wall. Her eyes were moist as she smiled in gratitude at his safe return. "Hi, little brother," she said.

They sat in the shade in the back yard that afternoon, Eric and Alison and Alison Two. Eric told them of the events of his journey.

Alison Two was as glad to see him, almost, as Alison was. Eric found himself thinking of her as another sister. But she wept when he told about Two and his treachery. She had thought of the other two clones as her brothers, Eric realized.

"It's over and finished," he said at last. "We just pick up and go on from here. I don't know yet what I'm going to tell Lt. Mitchell. I've got to think of something good."

But Alison Two wasn't listening. She was staring off into space beyond her companions. "And so the *things* that Dr. Swykert made will all be forgotten so very soon," she said.

"Alison—" Eric touched her hand. It was very cold. He saw the sunlight on the strands of gray in her hair.

# *Epilogue*

By early July, Alison Two was forty-five years old in appearance. From that point on, she aged incredibly quickly—adding years each day. Alison was with her constantly, trying to comfort her. They both knew she would not live more than two or three more weeks.

Her death came gently. She passed away in her sleep. It was Alison who found her. She had gone in to wake her friend, but her friend could not be wakened.

Eric noticed Alison had gone in to the guest room. When the silence became unbearable, he stepped to the door.

"Alison?"

She turned, tears streaming down her face.

"Is she—"

Alison nodded, but no words would come.

Later in the day, Alison had recovered from the initial shock. She and Eric sat in the gazebo. Alison was reading the twenty-third psalm. Eric sat quietly, not wanting her to be alone, but not wanting to say anything if she didn't want to talk.

"Do you really think she was human, Eric?" Alison asked suddenly. "Does it make any difference that she was a 'clone'?"

"I think she was human," replied Eric slowly. "But that's not all you're wondering is it?"

"No." She paused, not sure how to continue. "Was she—were they—spiritual?"

"I have to think so. I don't really see any reason they wouldn't have been."

"I'm glad you think so. That's what I was thinking—what I kept telling her. It was so hard for her to believe it, though. Dr. Swykert had treated them as 'things' for so long. They all thought of themselves that way."

"He did them a great injustice. If he'd only treated them as humans, Eric Two would never have felt he had so much to get even for."

They were silent for a moment. Then Eric continued. "Why all the doubt? You always seemed so convinced before. In fact, I thought you had convinced her. Didn't she—"

"Yes, I know. But now—well, I just wonder whether I was right. Now it's just—so final, or something. I hope I told her the right thing. She did believe—finally. I think our picnic made the difference."

"Picnic? What picnic?"

"While you were gone, we went on a picnic down by the creek. We talked a lot about life, about love, about

220

God. She wanted to believe so badly, but she didn't dare—not yet anyway."

"But she must have come around finally. That day at church—"

"Yes, finally she believed that she was real, that God loved her. That was an exciting day. I'm so glad she finally accepted what I'd been telling her. If she hadn't—"

"I know. I'm glad, too."

## *Thorne Twins* Adventure Books

## by Dayle Courtney

Available at your Christian bookstore or

# S†ANDARD
## PUBLISHING